Distraction . . .

The phone by the cash ▒▒▒▒▒▒▒▒▒▒▒▒, our captor, picked it up with his u▒▒▒ ▒▒▒▒▒ng. "Yo, *what*?"

From Keith's scowl, I judged that the hostage negotiator was telling him that there would be some delays in meeting Keith's demands, that coming up with a billion dollars by 5:15 might pose a problem, that sort of thing.

During their conversation, I heard something, a soft scraping noise on the ceiling above us. At first it sounded like a rat. But the more I listened to the deliberate scrape and pause, the more I was sure it was human. It was some SWAT guy working his way across the roof of the restaurant.

I wasn't too hot on the idea of a heavily armed SWAT team busting in the door. But the more I watched Keith, the more he scared me . . .

MORE MYSTERIES FROM THE
BERKLEY PUBLISHING GROUP...

BLUE PLATE SPECIAL

RUTH BIRMINGHAM

BERKLEY PRIME CRIME, NEW YORK

BLUE PLATE SPECIAL

A Berkley Prime Crime Book / published by arrangement with the author

PRINTING HISTORY
Berkley Prime Crime mass-market edition / September 2001

Visit our website at
www.penguinputnam.com

ISBN: 0-425-18186-3

Berkley Prime Crime Books are published
by The Berkley Publishing Group,
a division of Penguin Putnam Inc.,
375 Hudson Street, New York, New York 10014.
The name BERKLEY PRIME CRIME and the BERKLEY PRIME CRIME
design are trademarks belonging to Penguin Putnam Inc.

PRINTED IN THE UNITED STATES OF AMERICA

10 9 8 7 6 5 4 3 2 1

CHAPTER 1

S OME TRIGGER-HAPPY FOOL walks into a greasy spoon restaurant in the middle of Cabbagetown, pulls a gun, squeezes the trigger, a woman falls down dead. Obviously he killed her. It's a laydown, right?

Maybe, maybe not.

Truth is, people see what seems to make sense—which is not always the same as what actually happened. Magicians understand this: it's the basis of all illusion. You show one thing, but then you do another.

So you're asking, did I see the boy shoot Phyllis McClint in the Blind Pig Café? Strictly speaking, no. But I saw her bottle blond hair all spread out on the bloody floor, and I saw the boy with the gun standing over her. So in that sense I saw the same thing as everybody else. An illusion.

But do I know what happened?

I believe I do. *Now*, I believe I do.

For a girl in Cabbagetown, big hair *means* something.

Big Hair. You know what I'm talking about: the spray, the home dye job, the split ends, maybe some roots showing, the morning ritual of piling it all up, those volumes of upswooping, swirling, cascading, marvelous blondness!

In Cabbagetown big hair means more than it does out in the burbs. In Cabbagetown, big hair is the next best thing to *getting out*. And getting out is the great bugaboo, the unspeakable constant that's hung over every single soul in Cabbagetown for seventy-five years. Should I? Shouldn't I? *Can* I?

Cabbagetown is a funny place. It's one of those many unvisited, uncelebrated, hidden places in America where white people are poor and that's that. Nobody gives a hoot in hell about them. But what's different about Cabbagetown is that it has been under siege for ages and ages, yet still it has hung in there with a tough, hard, Scots resistance, hung in when most places would have just up and caved a long, long time ago.

To say you are from Cabbagetown is to say you have a certain kind of character.

Because what makes Cabbagetown special is that staying has a virtue here. Hunkering down, hanging in, taking it, dealing with it, absorbing the blow without whining—the hard, tough, stoic virtues of the Highland Scots—these things gave Cabbagetown a soul, made it a real place, when so many parts of America had gone plastic and airless, had become interchangeable parts in the great rootless plastic McDonald's juggernaut which is consuming the world. But those same virtues that separate Cabbagetown from the Valley Brooks and the Spring Harbors and the Cedarwood Estates and all the rest of the faceless gated tennis communities of America—those same virtues also made it a kind of prison.

If you live in Cabbagetown, big hair is a sort of declaration of independence, a tentative reaching out toward middleclassdom, toward the America that you see on TV, where people have new furniture and pretty clothes and cars that start right up when you turn the key. For the price of a can of hair spray and bottle of Clairol Ultra Blonde, you can state your intention or at least your wish, your hope, your small and hesitant dream of escape. But if you give up on toughness, on the sort of my-word-is-my-bond hardness of character which defines the place, what is left of you? What remains after you give up the Cabbagetown in your soul? That was the war that went on in every girl's mind—though she probably couldn't articulate it—when, with fingers trembling and pulse running a little hot, she picked up that first bottle of hair spray in the all-night drug store over on Memorial Drive.

And it was the argument, the war, that went on inside you as long as you stayed. If you stood up, if you got out, if you put your head up into the hurricane—well, there was no telling what might happen to you. You could get blown clean off the map, couldn't you?

Take Phyllis McClint, for instance. *She* had big hair. Big, big, *big* hair! And look what it got her.

There are only three kinds of clients. There are the pros, the bread-and-butter people. The pros are insurance companies and lawyers who need you to investigate car wrecks, bogus work-related disabilities, the usual small-time stuff that is at the root of most civil disputes. At Peachtree Investigations, we like the pros because they pay on time. The work is dull, dull, dull, yes. But money is a good thing.

Then you've got the assholes. People who start blood feuds with their neighbors over the breaking of some pointless neighborhood covenant, lawyers who want you to trump up evidence for their corporate clients so they can screw some little guy in a lawsuit, rich fat old men who think their ripe little twenty-five-year-old trophy wife is making it with the pool boy and so on. We put up with the assholes because their money spends just like everybody else's, but we have a separate billing rate for them which we call the "A Rate." "A Rate" clients get charged a 25 percent premium because we hate them.

Last, but not least, you have the nutty clients. They're people who want silly things investigated for silly reasons. We like nutty clients because they amuse us. Sometimes we charge them what we call the "N Rate," which is a discount of whatever we feel like giving them. Occasionally we don't charge them at all.

Esther Nixon is an "N Rate" client. She's a not particularly famous writer who harbored occasional quasi-paranoid fantasies on which she wanted us to take action. You've probably never heard of Esther because she writes under several pseudonyms. She is the romance novelist Victoria Cresswell. She's also the mystery novelists Sheila Corcoran and Sir Hubert Shackleford, and the legal thriller guy Walter Sorrells. Also the western writer Mike Dane. I'm sure there are more alter egos, but I don't know what they are.

Esther had called me up a while back and made a date to talk to me about an investigative matter. She wanted to meet at the Blind Pig, an old-fashioned café on Carroll Street in the East Atlanta neighborhood of Cabbagetown. I like the Blind Pig because it's one of the few greasy spoons left in downtown Atlanta, the kind of place where you still have waitresses that call you "hon" instead of introducing themselves with all this folderol about *Hello my name's Chaaaaaaad and I'll be your server today and the special for today is a Southwestern salad with radiccio and poblano peppers drenched in some weird-smelling crap you've never heard of and blah blah blah blah blah blah blah*.

Do you hate that as much as I do? Thanks but no thanks, Chaaaad.

No, at the Blind Pig the waitresses don't presume that you care what their names are, and they don't feel obliged to tell you about the special. If you want to know the special, it's written in blue chalk up on a blackboard hung over the grill behind the counter. The board says TODAY'S SPECIAL at the top, and at the bottom there's a faded ad for Pet Milk. There's no such thing as Pet Milk anymore, because Pet got bought up by an Italian dairy with a stupid, unpronounceable name. The Italian milk-marketing geniuses ditched a perfectly serviceable, homey, old-fashioned brand name for something that you and I can't pronounce and that probably doesn't even mean anything in Italian.

But hey, that's progress, right?

The blue plate special at the Blind Pig is usually something like fried chicken or chicken fried steak—something fried seven ways to Sunday, that much is certain—and you get two vegetables and cornbread and tea. *Sweet* tea. If you don't like sweet tea, don't go to the Blind Pig. Go to the place where Chaaaaaad will be your server. Go eat the southwestern salad, man.

Because Esther is an "N Rate" client, God forbid she should schedule a meeting at, say, lunch. No, Esther *must* meet me at midnight.

Being the punctual sort, I came into the Blind Pig at twelve on the dot. The waitress came over and I asked for tea. It came in a large brown plastic glass with a nubbly surface, and any time there was any danger of my running out, the waitress came by and refilled it from the yellow plastic jug she carried.

It was twelve forty-five by the time Esther Nixon finally breezed in. She is a large woman, large in all dimensions. With a personality to match.

"Sunny Childs!" she cried huskily to me. "Darling!" Everyone in the place stared. At six feet tall and a good two hundred pounds, she's not inconspicuous to begin with. Then she has the long gray wavy hair of an aging hippie hanging down to her hips. And finally there was the dress: it was a scarlet silk muumuu sort of thing embroidered with disturbingly detailed pictures of naked women playing Asian musical instruments while in the transports of some nameless ecstasy. It had just started to rain and there were dime-sized water splotches all over the dress. Her garb would have looked flamboyant in a Chinese whorehouse; but in a small down-home café, she wouldn't have gotten more stares if she had just descended from a spaceship.

I smiled painfully. I say painfully in part because promptness is one of those virtues I believe in with a bedrock piety, and partly because after all the tea I'd drunk waiting for her, my eyeballs were floating.

Esther gave me a huge bear hug (nearly squeezing the pee out of me—literally—in the process) then kiss-kiss-kissed me on the cheeks Russian style. "You will not," she intoned, *"believe!"* And I could tell that about twenty minutes of unbroken monologue was soon to follow.

I held up one finger. "Wait!" I commanded in the sort of loud, authoritarian voice you would use to keep your German Shepherd at heel. "Sit!"

Then I fled back to the toilet. You've been in the toilet at the Blind Pig. I don't mean literally, but you know the kind I mean: I'll spare you the blow-by-blow description, but let's just say it starts with cigarette burns on the toilet seat and goes from there. The kind of place where you sort of squat over the potty without letting any part of your anatomy even graze the seat, because God only knows what kind of mutant, flesh-eating bacteria has been growing and mutating there over the years.

I was squatting there, listening to the rain pouring outside the window, when I heard the first gunshot.

I have a carry permit and I own a little .38 with which I practice on a regular basis, so I know a gunshot when I hear it. And this was *loud.* Until you've heard gunshots inside a small room, you just have no idea how loud they are. And to my moderately trained ear, this was not some cheap girlie little gun either, a .25 or a .22. This was big-bore stuff. A .357 or a .44 or a nine-millimeter.

Bang, ba-bang! Then a pause. Adrenaline rushed through me. Outside the Blind Pig there was a flash of lightning, then the lights went out for about a second. As the lights came back on I heard another shot. *Bang!* Then nothing. Silence.

If you've ever gotten badly frightened while perched in that undignified position, you will know that your thigh muscles suddenly decide they don't want to hold you up anymore. I don't know if it was a case of my overactive curiosity getting the best of me or whether the thought of

letting my butt actually touch that foul seat was so unpleasant that I actually preferred the idea of going into a
room where someone had just fired a deadly weapon—
but, whatever the case, the next thing I knew I was pulling
up my pants and edging back into the restaurant to see
what had happened.

As soon as I did, I wanted to go back and sit down
again. I mean *really* sit.

Let me back up. The Blind Pig is one of those restaurants
that's built longways, so you come in the front door and
it's got a counter running down the right-hand wall and
a row of booths down the left, and then a handful of tables
in the back. The place was originally built back in the
twenties, but it was redecorated in the fifties. You've been
in a million places like the Blind Pig. Red formica, stain-
less steel, the cheapest kind of red plastic upholstery—the
kind that makes a nod toward leather, but only in a pro
forma way, and not with any intention to fool you that it
might actually *be* leather.

The cook was a beefy old guy with a sour face and a
greasy comb-over and an undershot chin and jailhouse
tattoos on his forearms. He was crouched on the floor
behind the counter, as was the waitress, a fleshy, pale
woman with a lot of eye makeup and a big pile of dead
black hair.

The guy with the gun was young. A kid, really. He had
a bad complexion and bad teeth, pale skin. He was a white
kid, but decked out in full rap star regalia: the usual baggy
T-shirt that said MASTER P on the front, khakis that hung
halfway down his butt so you could see two inches of
plain white boxer shorts over the top, his hair done up in
lots of limp little braids with different-colored rubber
bands on the ends, black Doc Martens. He also had a gold
tooth cap with a star cut into it. A real genius, you could
tell. But the main thing you noticed was the gun, a big
shiny automatic pistol that was pointing directly at the
dead woman.

Not that I took her pulse or anything, but it was obvious she was gone.

The victim was about my age, I'd say. Midthirties. Big hair. Lots and lots and *lots* of swirling, curling, sprawling, sprayed, dyed blond hair. Other than the hair, the main thing you noticed about her was that she had what they used to call a generous figure. Not precisely fat, but maybe a little on the Rubenesque side—at least by the standards thrust on us by *Vogue* magazine.

And then, of course, there was the blood. It wasn't just a little blood, either. The blood had sprayed around the room like it had come out of a hose. The gunshots had gone off less than half a minute before I left the bathroom—but he'd hit her in the neck, must have torn out the carotid artery because she wasn't even moving. And the blood? *Quarts* of blood. Quarts! On the tables, on the counter, on the BLUE PLATE SPECIAL sign, on the ceiling. Until you see it, you can hardly imagine what happens when you tear open a big artery like that. It's like a fire hose; it just goes everywhere. There were even drops of it still sizzling on the grill. You have *no* idea how horrible it was.

The kid saw me then, and he started screaming. "Get back in here! Get down! Sit yo' boo-tey down or I'll kill you, you dumb ho!" He went on like that, a white guy but with this silly black accent, like he'd learned to talk from watching *Yo! MTV Raps.*

So the rap star came running to the back of the restaurant and he grabbed me and shoved me into an empty booth, and then he ran back down to the end of the counter where the register was, tracking the dead woman's blood with his boots.

"Gimme da money!" He pointed the gun at the grill man. "Give me the money, bi-yetch!" The grill man stood up shakily. He had a stubble of dark beard, but underneath his skin was dead white, giving him a strange gray coloring. He hit a button on the register, scooped out the money, put it on the counter.

"Not *that* money!" The kid was screaming at the top of his lungs, like the grill man was deaf. "You know what I'm talking about!"

"Huh?" the grill man said.

"The money in the box, you know wha' I'm saying? I wants the money in the box!"

The grill man looked at the kid, and put both hands up on his gray face, pressing his palms together like he was trying to squeeze his own head flat. Finally he said, "Son, I don't know what box you talking about."

"The box, bi-yetch! I wants the money in the box!

"I—"

"The *egg* box!"

"The egg box." The grill man was staring at the kid with the gun with a sick, confused look on his face.

"The egg box! The egg box!"

The kid pointed his gun at a cardboard box that was lying on the floor beside the table with the milkshake machine on it.

"*This* egg box?" The grill man, looking slightly confused, held up the cardboard box. It said A&M EGGS on the side in red letters.

"Give it up! Turn it over!" The boy was shaking, he was so hyped up, and he was waving the gun around.

The grill man held the box up over the counter, then turned the box over. It seemed like slow motion, everybody waiting for a bunch of money to fall out. The boy was so certain that there was money in the box, that it almost had the feel of a magic trick when all that came out was a cascade of eggs, falling on the counter and shattering. The yolks seemed unnaturally yellow as they mixed with the splatters of red blood and the whites of the shells, and then started leaking down the front of the counter.

The kid stared at the eggs like he couldn't believe what had happened, like some article of deep faith in his life had just been exposed as a pure sham. There was a country music song playing on the juke box, that old Vern

Gosdin song, "Chiseled In Stone." We must have listened to an entire verse of the song and half the chorus while everybody stared at those eggs.

The boy leapt over the counter and jammed the gun in the grill man's face.

"I just—" The grill man still had this stunned look on his face. "I just . . . look, son, I give you all the money in the till, I don't . . . I got a little money in my . . ." He fished out his wallet, took out a mess of bills and dropped them on top of the eggs.

The boy glared at him furiously. "You think you can hose me, bi-yetch? You think that? Huh?" He put the gun up against the grill man's gray face and pulled back the hammer.

There's no telling what might have happened next. But it didn't—because at that moment there was a screeching noise outside as two cop cars skidded to a stop on the curb and a bunch of patrol officers jumped out, guns in their hands.

The kid turned, pointed his gun at the cops through the plate glass, and when men in blue ducked behind the doors of their cars, the kid jerked the cord on a set of Venetian blinds. The blinds went down with a whispering, jangling noise and then we couldn't see anything out the front window.

"Come'ere!" the kid screamed at me.

I got up on wobbly legs and I walked down the aisle, trying not to look at the dead woman on the floor. But I could feel her blood, sticky on my shoes. When I got to the front, the kid grabbed me around the neck, jerked open the door, and jammed the gun against my head.

"Get back!" he screamed at the police. The front sight of his pistol was jabbing painfully into the bone right behind my ear. "Get back or I'ma cap this ho!"

The cops were all around us. "Give it up, dude!" one of the cops yelled. He was wearing mirrored wrap-around sunglasses, pointing a gun, it seemed, right at my forehead.

"Be cool," another cop said.

"Get back or everybody gonna die!" the kid screamed. He followed that up with a stream of enthusiastic but un-inventive cussing, then ducked back inside the Blind Pig, slammed the door shut, and locked the dead bolt. A little bell over the door tinkled merrily.

The kid shoved me down the aisle in the middle of the café until we reached a plywood door in the back. He peeped through the door, but I guess he saw cops because he did some more cussing and yelling, then slammed the door shut. A chain with a lock dangling off of it hung from the handle. The kid wrapped the chain through the handle, shoved it through a U-shaped piece of steel screwed to the wall, then closed the lock so that no one could get in or out the back door. When he was done, he shoved me in the direction of counter.

"Sit yo ass down," he said. "I gots to think."

CHAPTER 2

CABBAGETOWN IS A funny place. It's a little neighborhood on the crummy side of Atlanta, just south of Decatur Street and North of Memorial, that surrounds the old Fulton Bag & Cotton Mill. Way back, around the turn of the century, there had been a labor shortage in the city and so the owners had sent a man up to Appalachia, where he recruited a whole flock of hillbillies to come down and work for him at the mill. The owners set up their own little neighborhood right on the outskirts of Atlanta, building themselves what was in effect an old-fashioned mill town. Houses and stores were all owned by the mill.

It was a poor community—textile workers have long been the worst-paid industrial workers in the world—and the smell of cabbage wafting through the air at night gave the neighborhood its name.

Over the years the mill continued to provide employment to the same group of families living in the neighborhood. The entire Cabbagetown area remained a sort of *cordon sanitaire*, even as the city grew to engulf the area and the working-class white folks in surrounding neighborhoods abandoned their homes to blacks, Cabbagetown continued as an enclave not only of white folks, but of white folks who carried on the mores and speech of the North Carolina hills.

The mill closed sometime around 1970, but the same group of families continued to live in the area. Many Cabbagetowners were third and even fourth generation residents, and the insularity and cohesiveness of the neighborhood kept the neighborhood whole when virtually every other working-class white neighborhood in the city of Atlanta proper had disappeared.

By the time the cotton mill shut down, Atlanta had swallowed Cabbagetown completely. It had become an "inner city" neighborhood. Only, contrary to the usual stereotype, it was white. Like the black neighborhoods around it, Cabbagetown ran into trouble once the jobs dried up. A large proportion of the adult population went on welfare, drugs were rampant, drinking—which had always been a feature of Cabbagetown—became more of a problem.

In the past decade downtown Atlanta has finally been rediscovered by the middle class. Tired of the longest commutes on the planet, the bleakness of suburban life, and so on, the middle class has been creeping southward toward—and even beyond—the heart of the city. With a limited amount of space and a housing stock which hasn't risen significantly since the 1960s, downtown real estate has skyrocketed. Old neighborhoods, many of them gone to rack and ruin, have been—or are being—gentrified. It's the same old pattern: first come the artists and musicians and students. Next come the young couples and the owners of small businesses catering to downtown industries: advertising, video production, copy shops, and the like. The price of real estate rises, old people looking to retire or going into nursing homes sell out, tax assessments rise, locals can't afford to continue living in the neighborhood, and the original population gets displaced.

Once the best neighborhoods and the ones closest to the white north side of town had been cherry-picked, the inexorable process pushed on. Inevitably things caught up with Cabbagetown.

The old bag mill was gutted and a developer began turning it into condominiums. And buyers and speculators, piecemeal, began picking up the little white mill houses on the cheap, hanging fancy new doors, sprucing up the porches and yards, adding central air, and laying down hardwood floors.

As I would begin to understand, this murder was all about Cabbagetown—about what it once was, about what it was becoming.

"Rule One." The kid strutted up and down the room. "Rule One, nobody talks. If I see anybody talk to anybody else, they ass be dead. Rule Two. They is only one rule." The kid seemed pleased with himself, thinking he was one of those witty villains in a movie.

I sat on a stool at the counter, my heart thumping in my rib cage, and didn't move. No one else in the room moved either.

Outside, somebody started talking to the kid through a megaphone, but the stereo was playing Garth Brooks and you couldn't make out what the megaphone person was saying.

"A'ight, word up," the kid with the gun said loudly to the people in the café. "Here's where we at. We surrounded. Y'all fools is hostages. Y'all piss me off, I'ma put a cap in you, you know what I'm saying?" And then he did a slow strut up the aisle, a limping pimp roll like he was auditioning for a role in *Shaft,* pointing the gun at people as he went. "Yeeeeeaah," he said, pointing the gun and leering at somebody. "Thass right. Yeeeeah."

If you'd seen it in a movie, it would have seemed pretty lame, this white kid trying to act like some MTV super pimp. But when it was a real gun and a real woman lying dead on the floor, it didn't seem funny at all. Grotesque is the word that springs to mind.

Finally the kid sat down at the counter. "A'ight," he said. "A'ight."

"All right, *what*?" the waitress said uneasily. She was about fifty, but her hair was stone black. I don't think it was dyed; she was just one of those people whose hair never grays, and who, as a result, looks weirder and weirder as the years go by.

"Yo, lemme get a menu."

The waitress looked at him resentfully. "A *menu*? Boy, you out your mind." She had the sort of swallowed, glottal-sounding vowels that you only heard in East Tennessee, Western North Carolina, Kentucky. It's how the old residents of Cabbagetown still talked.

The kid looked at her. "What's your name?"

"Loretta Lynn."

"Don't be playing me, bi-yetch," the boy said.

"That's my name, by God," the waitress said. "Loretta Lynn Jones."

The boy grinned, showing off his foolish gold tooth with the star cut in it. "Man, that's some country-ass shit, ain't it?" Then he grabbed a menu and looked through it for a minute. "A'ight. I wants me three eggs scrambled hard. Not loose. Hard. I don't want no snot-feeling eggs. Word? If I gets one little piece of that snotty feeling stuff, I'ma cap yo ass."

The waitress looked back at him stonily, then looked around the room. "What's wrong with this boy?" she said. "Used to be we had good people here in Cabbagetown. Hardworking? Decent? Churchgoing? Maybe drank a little come Sat'dy night, but I don't reckon nobody'd hold that against them. Now all these moe-rons and crackheads and trash coming around. What's the point being here? We was like family! Now look at us."

The kid narrowed his eyes. "Shut up, ho. Remember Rule One? Huh?" Then he went back to the menu. "Yeaaahh. And I wants me some sausage. Patty sausage not no *link* sausage. And four pieces of toast. Y'all gots raisin toast?"

Loretta Lynn looked disgusted. "*No,* we ain't got no raisin toast."

"What toast y'all gots?"

"White."

"White. What else?"

"White. I said."

The kid looked incredulous. "That's *it*? White? Y'all ain't got no wheat? Or either no rye or nothing?"

"White."

"Pumpernickel?"

The waitress put her hands on her ample hips. "White."

"Well, dog. Gimme white toast." He wrinkled up his brow. "Uhhh. Yeah, gimme a waffle too. With some whipped cream on it. And blueberries. And chocolate syrup. And a T-bone steak. Y'all got a T-bone steak?"

"Uh-huh."

The waitress stood there for a while, and the megaphone droned on outside, and Garth Brooks sang another of his crappy songs.

"Yo!" the kid said finally. "Make the food or I'ma slap yo booty into the middle of next week!"

"You just gonna sit there, eat all that food while that lady you shot's just a-laying there on the floor?"

The kid looked over his shoulder at the dead woman, as though he just noticed her. "I ain't *shot* that lady," he said.

Curiosity again: I couldn't help poking in. "Then who did?" I said.

The kid looked over at me, gave me a long, lingering up-and-down the body gaze. "I don't know, baby," he said with a big innocent shrug. "Wasn't me."

"Oh," I said. "You just walked in here and fired off half a clip and she fell dead accidentally."

He shrugged. "I ain't shot nobody. Word." He pointed his gun at the grill man with the few strands of hair greased across his bald head. "Yo! Comb-Over! Let's get on it, dog."

The grill man got busy suddenly, looking like he was glad to have something to do.

I don't know what it is about me, but it's no accident I ended up being a PI. There's something deep inside me that's driven to observe things. First I studied the kid with the gun. Once I felt like I had a good picture of him in my mind, I started looking around the room, counting how many people there were, where they were located, trying to record everything about the event in my mind.

There were about a dozen people in the room. At the first booth along the wall was a pretty but hard-faced girl with lank brown hair and about three times the recommended daily allowance of eyeliner. Other than the bonus dose of eyeliner though, no makeup. Her bony shoulders poked out of the torn-off sleeves of a Harley Davidson T-shirt. Sitting across from her was a large handsome young man with hair cut long in the back and short on the sides. He was very muscular, but without a lot of definition: you could see he was one of these weight lifter types who was rapidly on the road to becoming an old guy with a jumbo beer belly. The weight lifter looked at the kid truculently, but didn't speak.

At the next booth sat another couple. They couldn't have been more different from their neighbors. He was an extremely handsome guy with fashionable black-framed eyeglasses that had a barely visible blue tint and a buzz cut and a black knit shirt that buttoned up to the neck. His only jewelry was a heavy gold wedding band on his left hand. His wife—I used my vast deductive powers to figure out that they were married based on the matching ring she wore—was also attractive in a boho-cum-professional sort of way: she wore the unnecessarily bright red lipstick and black clothes of the boho, but the gym-trim figure and the glossy black pageboy told me she was a member of the professional classes. Her skin was creamy and her mouth wide. I guessed her to be Jewish, while the husband looked pure-bone WASP, a good southern boy gone all arty-farty on his nice Baptist parents.

At the next table was a man of about forty wearing a shiny gold six-button suit and a white shirt with gold trimmed french cuffs. His sandy hair had a weird sort of Hair Club for Men quality to it. I couldn't tell if it was a toup or if it was just the copious amount of glop he'd sprayed in his hair that gave it its strangely unnatural sheen. Based on the ensemble, he was either gay or a Pentecostal minister. The fact that he had his eyes closed and his hands clasped together and that his lips were moving inaudibly led me to guess the latter. But you never knew. A drop of what I assumed was the dead woman's blood glistened on his upper lip.

At the next table were two old couples, Cabbagetown locals for certain. All four of them were hatchet-faced, stoic-looking people. Both old men wore overalls. The women wore the regulation polyester of old ladies on tight budgets. They kept their eyes on the table and didn't move. One of the men had tears running down his face, but otherwise they just looked grim and expressionless.

I've already mentioned my client, Esther Nixon, who sat in a booth, her back to the action, head turned so she could see. She alone seemed unmoved by the scene. In fact, she appeared rather interested.

I take it back. There was one other person who didn't seem frightened. Sitting by himself at a two-person table near the front was a small fat man wearing a pair of overalls and thick glasses with plastic frames that were held together with white surgical tape. He had a childlike expression on his face, and what we used to call "liver lips" when I was a kid—his lips weren't just large, but were loose and moist, the kind of lips that gave a person a bovine, idiotic look. He was watching the robbery unfold like it was a show on TV. There was a lot of food in front of him, and periodically he would put something in his mouth and chew it with his mouth open, the half-chewed food shifting around on full display.

Everyone was hunkered down, as much of their bodies sheltered under their tables as they could manage.

After a minute I heard someone clear their throat loudly.

The kid turned around. The guy with the fashionable glasses put a big smile on his face, the smile of a guy who believes that all women love him and that all men think he's really cool. "Hey look, man," the guy with the fashionable glasses said. His voice was cheery, but with a condescending edge. "I'm going to jump in here and offer a little free advice . . ."

"You *what*?"

The guy with the fashionable glasses stood up slowly, then put out his hand as though to shake. The kid just stared at him, his limp little braids hanging in his eyes. Finally the fashionable guy lowered his hand. "Anyway, I'm Patrick. How you doing, man. I live in the neighborhood. And, anyway, what I was thinking is maybe before this whole thing gets all out of whack, maybe it would be good if you had somebody to sort of be a go-between. Between you and the cops? It's kind of hard to hear in here and so I was thinking if you had like a representative who could help you articulate what you wanted and maybe help to—"

"Is it something wrong with your ears, dude?" the kid said, eyes widening with pretend surprise. "Did I not explain Rule One about two minutes ago?"

"Nah, nah, man, I don't mean I'm volunteering or whatever. It's just that—"

The kid stood up and hit the fashionable guy, Patrick, in the head with the butt of his gun.

"Ow! Man! What the . . ." The young man's fashionable glasses flew across the room. He covered his head with his hands, a stunned look on his face.

"Hey dumb-ass." It was the hard-faced girl with all the eyeliner, the one sitting at the next table. "Sit your fool self down before he shoots you."

"Listen up, y'all," the kid said. "Rule One ain't no joke.

Nobody talks. Not unless I axe 'em a direct question."

Patrick stumbled backwards, sat down with an uncomprehending look on his face. His wife hissed under her breath at him. "I *told* you, Patrick."

"He just hit me in the head, Connie!" the young man returned. "The least you could do is feign a tiny shred of sympathy."

She scowled but then dipped her napkin in her water and reached across the table to dab at the oozing wound on his forehead. When she touched him, though, he jerked away from her.

As the doughy waitress, Loretta Lynn, set two heaping plates in front of the kid, the jukebox went quiet. Suddenly we could hear the megaphone outside. "Hello! Hello in there. This is Major Jarvis Drummond of the Atlanta Police Department. We need to talk."

The kid stood up, walked to the door, poked his gun out, waved it in the air. "I'm trying to eat me some breakfast, y'all!" he screamed. "Next bi-yetch talks through that megaphone, I'ma cap one of my peoples."

Then he shut the door and did his *Yo! MTV Raps* strut back to the counter, a small self-satisfied smirk on his face. "Just pimping, baby," he said, winking at me. "Got to represent. Yeeeeeah. The Superstar just be pimping." But I could see his hands were trembling slightly.

He sat next to me, shoved the gun into the waist of his pants, then slathered his eggs with ketchup. He stabbed a piece of egg with his fork, put it in his mouth, chewed, then finally spit it back out, and slumped over in his stool.

"You *are* going to have to do something," I said softly. "Otherwise the cops will kill you."

"I ain't kill that lady," he mumbled. "I ain't."

"Then who did?"

He didn't answer. There was a long, accusatory silence in the restaurant. The kid threw his fork down on the plate. It rattled loudly.

"Don't nobody say I killed that lady! Don't nobody say it or I'll kill you."

There was a long, fearful silence.

Finally I leaned toward the kid. "Let's say that's true," I said. I was trying to keep my voice soft, not coming on like a know-it-all, but just like I was talking to a friend in a bar. "You can't stay here forever, right?"

"So?"

So, I wasn't sure what. I guess I was hoping he'd run out the back door or something, and leave us alone.

"If I may." Everyone turned to look. It was Esther Nixon, strolling up the aisle, her hands spread like a Catholic priest giving the benediction.

"Who the hell is you?"

"Esther Nixon," she said imperiously. "The writer." As though this moron would have heard of her. The guy probably thought Shakespeare was an alternative rock band.

He gave her the what-planet-are-you-from? expression. But he seemed so startled by her that he didn't do anything to silence her. "Did I not just explain about Rule One? Shit! Y'all peoples deaf!"

"Please. One moment," Esther said. "It's not as though I'm discussing escape plans with my fellow hostages. Yes? So let us engage in a bit of Socratic exchange, my dear."

The kid kept staring at her.

"First, young man, a proposition. The police *will* come in here eventually. Yes? Whether you surrender or escape or get shot by some nice SWAT officer, the police will eventually take control. And when they do, naturally, they shall assume that you did this. Correct?"

The boy looked uneasily at the dead woman. "But I *ain't*." He had a whiny, pleading quality in his voice.

Esther Nixon smiled pityingly at him. "My dear lad, that is entirely beside the point."

"So what I'm gonna do?"

"Suppose," Esther said, "that you are, in fact, not guilty of this murder."

"That's what I'm *saying*."

"Further, suppose that within these four walls was not only the real murderer, but also a private investigator of great skill and renown."

"Oh come on, Esther," I said softly.

Esther Nixon silenced me with a grand sweep of her hand, her silk dress rustling softly. "Suppose, young man, that both these things were true. What would seem to be the logical thing to do?"

The kid looked at her blankly.

"Come now, young man!" Esther Nixon clapped her hands together. "Quickly! Time flies like the wind!"

"Uh. I guess if the detective could, like, you know . . ."

"Investigate?" Esther said. "Hm?"

The boy nodded dully. "Yeah. Investigate."

Esther Nixon smiled triumphantly. "*Exactemente!* Investigate."

"Yeah, but I don't see no brilliant master detective hanging around all up in here."

"Ah! My dear, but how wrong you are." She smiled brightly, waved her hand at me. "Permit me to introduce Atlanta's finest investigative intellect, Sunny Childs."

He looked at me dubiously. "Lemme think for a minute."

"After Miss Childs concludes her investigation, and deduces the real killer, she will then produce an affidavit for the police identifying the killer, thereby eliminating any potential charges against you."

"Huh?"

"I mean to say, you would then be charged, at most, with something like, oh, aggravated mayhem, possession of a firearm, something like that. An affidavit from a licensed private detective, young man, that's your get-out-of-jail-free card. An affidavit."

I couldn't believe the temerity she had, cooking up something this patently ridiculous. Surely this kid didn't think he could walk out of this place without being charged with armed robbery and murder.

"Lemme *think*!" the kid said. He walked up to the front window and peeped out through the blinds.

"Are you crazy?" I whispered to Esther. "This idiot was right here in plain view when he shot her."

"Did *you* see it?" Esther whispered back.

I shook my head.

"Neither did I, Sunny." She continued to smile. "Anyway, the point is, your 'investigation' will keep everyone occupied and focused, and it will help to kill time until the police hostage negotiators have ground him down. That way, perhaps we'll manage to get out of here before he shoots someone else."

Put that way, it didn't sound entirely stupid. "A charade," I whispered.

"A charade, yes." She pronounced the word French style, sha-ROD.

The kid came back from the window. Turning to me, he said, "A'ight, lady, how you gonna do this?"

I swallowed. "Well, hm. I guess I'd start by interviewing everybody in the room. See who saw what."

The kid looked thoughtful.

Something occurred to me then, something that not only made sense under the goofy logic of the charade investigation but also under the notion that this was a way of getting myself out of a dangerous situation unscathed. "Obviously, I couldn't really talk to them where you could listen to them. They'd have to be free to speak openly to me about what they saw."

"It's a storage room back there," the doughy waitress said helpfully. "You could talk to folks in there. Don't have no door to the outside, so it ain't like nobody could sneak out of it or nothing."

The kid walked down to where the waitress had been pointing, opened a large green-painted metal door, looked in, and squinted for a few moments. "A'ight," he said to me. "But I hear you rummaging around in here, getting cute, I'ma cap you."

"Fair enough," I said. Then, after a pause, I added, "By the way, now that you're my client, what do I call you?"

He looked around the room for a minute, then gave me a big wink. "Call me Superstar, baby."

CHAPTER 3

"SAY. SAY, MAN."

It was the grill man, the beefy guy with the comb-over and the jailhouse tattoos.

The kid looked over at him, annoyed. "What!"

"Say, man. I got a prostrate problem."

"Huh?" The kid's mouth hung open, a thin braid with a green rubber band around the end swinging slowly in front of his face. Pro*strate* or pro*state,* the kid still probably had no idea what he was talking about.

The grill man lowered his voice to a whisper. "I got to *go,* son. Bad."

"Bad enough to get shot over?"

The grill man stared hard at the kid, then looked away.

"What if I talk to him first?" I said. "You let him go to the bathroom, then I talk to him."

The kid looked around the room as though challenging everybody. "Who's the man?"

"Pardon?" I said.

"Who da man?"

"Uh," I said. "*You're* the man?"

"Straight up. *I'm* the man." He slapped his chest, then pointed the gun at the grill man. "You gonna have to wait." He swiveled the gun toward the waitress, holding it sideways, his pinky finger sticking up in the air. That's how the thugs do it on TV now. Thug chic—ain't it grand? "A'ight then. Talk to *her*. She seen what happened."

"Okay, Loretta Lynn," I said. "Let's do it."

The waitress and I walked back to the green door and entered a small, close room that smelled of ancient meat and cigarette smoke. It was lit by a single bare bulb hanging from the middle of the ceiling. Along one wall were stacks of cardboard boxes—toilet paper, plastic cups, things like that. On the opposite wall were shelves full of cereal, loaves of bread, and bags of flour.

I pulled two cardboard boxes out into the middle of the room, sat on one of them. Loretta Lynn Jones sat across from me, pulling out a cigarette with trembling fingers and lighting it immediately. I was still trying to decide whether or not she dyed her big pile of peculiarly black hair. She was a soft woman with eyebrows that had been plucked so aggressively that only a few stray hairs remained, giving her a constant look of mild bewilderment.

"Lord, Lord, Lord," she said, shaking her head. "Didn't use to be like this around here."

"Oh?" I felt no particular pressure to ferret anything out. As far as I was concerned, I was just killing time.

"My great granddaddy come to Cabbagetown eighty, ninety years ago. Used to be hardworking folks here, didn't have no time to get in no trouble."

"This kid," I said. "Superstar or whatever his name is— is he from around here?"

"Never seen him." She blew out a long stream of smoke. "Seen plenty like him, though. No sense, all niggery-acting. Makes you sick."

"Mm," I said.

"Not that I got nothing against the coloreds, don't get me wrong. I ain't prejudice against nobody. But it ain't natural for no white boy to go around talking colored, dressing colored, acting colored. It ain't natural."

The room was quiet for a moment. I could hear the

crackle of the burning tobacco as Loretta Lynn drew on her cigarette.

"Nah," Loretta Lynn said, "Cabbagetown's done for. You see a thing like this, it's just one more nail in the coffin."

"I got the impression the neighborhood was turning around," I said.

Loretta Lynn's shoulders moved up and down like she was laughing, but no noise came out of her mouth. "Turning around? Meaning what? Rich folks moving in so all us poor white trash can't afford to live here no more? Nah, this place used to be something you could put your finger on. It may of been a shithole, but it was a shithole that you knew what it was. I used to be proud to know my neighbors, know who I went to church with. You knew everybody else, you knew their mama and their daddy, you knew everything about everybody. It was just like a little bitty old town." She finished her cigarette, dropped it on the floor, and ground it out with her white nurse's shoe. "You see that couple, the fellow that this here Superstar idiot hit upside the head? I don't know their names, much less who was their mama and daddy. Them two bought old Mr. Sheily's place, Jim Sheily, Sr., the one had the missing thumb? They bought his place after he passed. He's a artist or whatever. Her, she works downtown. They don't talk to nobody, they don't play with the kids, they don't come to church around here. What kind of people are they? I don't even know."

Superstar poked his head around the door, did a little shimmy with his shoulders that he'd probably seen in some Puff Daddy video. "Yo, baby. Whass up? She telling it straight?"

"We're just getting started," I said.

Superstar narrowed his eyes, and pointed his gun at the waitress. "Lady, you better keep it real, a'ight?"

"Hey," I said. "Come on, Superstar. I need some space here or I won't get anywhere."

"Supahstah! Yeeeeahhh. He's a playah!" Another broad wink and the kid retreated out the door.

Loretta Lynn shook her head again. "Pitiful," she said.

"So I guess we better get started. Just for appearances."

The waitress didn't seem to be listening to me though. She just picked up right where she'd left off. "They ain't nobody left in Cabbagetown except old people and a few shiftless folks on welfare or some kind of trumped-up disability. Everybody with any get-up-and-go has done got up and went."

"How come you stayed?" I said.

"I been working here all my life. Don't know nothing else. This here's my home." For the first time she looked up, her eyes burning into mine. "Can you imagine what it's like watching your whole world just drain away like this? I don't know who I hate more, moe-rons like this Superstar fool, or folks like that artist fellow and his snotty wife. Either way, they tearing this place down. Another ten years, if the coloreds don't take over, it's gonna be like everywhere else in this city, a bunch of people don't even know they neighbor's names."

"Yeah," I said. "You could be right. But . . . if I could change the subject, did you see this kid shoot the woman?"

"Phyllis McClint."

"I'm sorry?"

"Phyllis McClint. She's got a name. Her daddy used to be a foreman down at the mill. He was a big man around here. She turned out to be a lot like him."

"Oh?"

"She's head of POCA."

"Polka?"

"Not like the dance. P-O-C-A. People of Cabbagetown Alliance." She fished another cigarette out of her pack and put it in her mouth but didn't light it. "It's like a neighborhood association."

"Okay. But did he shoot her?"

The waitress looked at me like I was crazy. "Of course

he shot her. Silly-ass little son of a bitch, shot her for nothing."

"You saw it?"

"Well." Loretta Lynn shrugged as though this were not an important matter. "Not exactly."

"What exactly *did* you see?"

"Well, it was raining, right? And I seen him come in. Superstar, or whatever his name is, I mean. He drug out that big old gun, and I'm standing next to the register, and he yells, you know, gimme the F-this F-that money, you F-this F-that. Calls me a whore. I ought to of hit him with a doggone frying pan. Then he shoots a few shots in the ceiling. Then lightning hit somewhere? Ka-POW! The lightning makes the lights go out for a second, so I hit the deck. Then the lights come on and I hear him shoot."

"So you didn't actually *see* him shoot her."

She looked vaguely offended. "I *heard* the shot, by God! Who else could it have been? He's the only one standing there with a gun."

"How many shots did you hear?" I said. "Four? Five?"

"How in the samhill would I know? All's I know, he shot a bunch of times at the ceiling, then after that I only heard one more shot."

I nodded. That jibed with the way I'd heard it from the bathroom.

"We done?" the waitress said.

I shook my head. "Do me a favor, keep talking."

"About what?"

"Doesn't matter."

Loretta Lynn looked at me curiously. I slid my hand inside the jacket of my pocket. "You don't think I actually came back here because I'm trying to prove he didn't kill that woman, do you?" I held up a cell phone in my hand.

Loretta Lynn blinked, then smiled thinly. "I hope you ain't too smart for you own good," she said. Then she started talking about something innocuous that had happened to her earlier in the day.

I dialed 911. "Hello? My name is Sunny Childs. I'm inside the Blind Pig. Where the hostage thing is happening."

"Hold please," the operator said. "I want to transfer you to somebody." There were some clicks and then a man's voice. "Major Drummond here. Who am I speaking to?"

I whispered. "My name's Sunny Childs. I'm a private investigator."

A brief pause. "Wait. I recognize your name. You're that gal that works for Gunnar Brushwood?"

"Yessir."

"Outstanding." Major Drummond had an exaggerated military lilt to his voice. "You in a position to give me a sit rep?"

"Sit rep?"

"Situation report."

"Oh. Yessir. One robber. Goes by the street name of Superstar. Male white, age approximately twenty, several tattoos. Blue shirt, baggy khakis, brown hair down to his shoulders in braids with little colored rubber bands on the ends. He's armed with a pistol. I think it's a SIG. Fourteen hostages. He has locked the back door with a substantial chain. I'm in a storage room, but only temporarily so I can't talk long. We've got one casualty."

"Status?"

"Dead. Her name is Phyllis McClint. A Cabbagetown local."

"You're sure she's dead?"

"Absolutely."

"Does he have any other weapons? Knife, grenade, bomb, anything?"

"Not that I've seen."

I heard footsteps outside the room. "Gotta go," I said. I shoved the cell phone back in my pocket.

Loretta Lynn was still talking.

"You can't imagine how it feels," she said, "when everything you know is dying."

Superstar put his head around the corner. "Y'all done?"

I nodded. "I believe so."

"Who's next?" he said.

I walked out into the room looked around. "You," I said finally. "I want to hear *your* story."

CHAPTER 4

"EVEN WHEN I was a kid," Superstar said, jiving around in front of me with this sly little grin, "the females loved me."

"Uh, nothing personal," I said, "but this isn't *Entertainment Tonight*. I'm not looking for your life story. I just want to know what happened here."

The kid's face fell a little, then went hard. He was standing halfway into the freezer, peeping out while we talked so he could keep an eye on the other hostages. "You disrespecting me? Huh? Huh, bi-yetch?"

"I'm just doing my job," I said. "Remember? There are a bunch of cops out there waiting for a chance to take you down. I'm trying to help you. Again, nothing personal, but it's not because I love you, it's not because you're so suave and debonaire. I just want this situation resolved peacefully."

"Well, I done told you! I ain't shot that lady."

I nodded, trying to be patient. "I understand. You've made that very clear. But what I want is a little more detail. Step by step. You open the door, then what?"

"Well. See, I'm kind of between work right now? I was staying with my homey, Jay-Rock? But he got evicted. So I'm like on the street right now, you know what I'm saying? Temporarily. Been staying up at the Mission on Ponce de Leon. Anyway, what happened, I met this dude on the street today. He told me about how this restaurant, the Blind Pig, they kept a lot of cash money around. Said he been a dishwasher here once. And he said he'd tell me how to get paid if I wanted. Said he'd split the take half and half."

"What do you mean? You do all the work and he gets half the money?"

"Well, you know . . ." Superstar's eyes flicked around anxiously, like I'd tactlessly exposed his questionable aptitude as a criminal. "I mean I wouldn't go for no fifty-fifty. I went for eighty, uh, uh . . ."

"Eighty-twenty?"

"Eighty-twenty. Yeah." The kid seemed relieved that I'd solved his mathematical conundrum. "So he's like, yeaaah. 'Cause he know I'm a player, right? So he give me this gun. Anyway, he told me they don't got no safe here. They puts the money in a egg box behind the counter. Said they usually makes the deposit to the night deposit box at like 1 A.M. So right now be when they gots the maximum cash on hand."

"And who was this guy?"

"Some dude."

"Just . . . some dude. Do you know this guy?"

"Nah. He just another player that's temporarily staying at the Mission."

"You know his name?"

"John."

"John what?"

"John . . . uh . . . Smiff."

"You serious? He said his name was John Smith? And you *believed* that?"

"Yo, you axing me, I'm telling you."

"And he loaned you the gun? Or gave it to you?"

Superstar shrugged. "I guess he just loaned it to me."

The thing that struck me as odd about the story was that the weapon he was carrying—a SIG, as best I could tell—was a pretty high-end pistol. It probably retailed for about seven or eight hundred bucks. He could have pawned the gun for more money than he was liable to get holding up a restaurant.

He leaned closer to me, as though letting me in on a confidence. "Also? Dude said this ain't really a holdup."

"Meaning what?"

"It's like a scam."

"A scam."

"Yeah. Dude that give me the gun say he know the owner of this place. What happen, the owner store up all his cash receipts in this box, then he get somebody to heist it. Split up the money four ways. Then he make a insurance claim. Get all his money back, plus his cut, plus he don't even have to pay no income tax on it."

I frowned. "Yeah but I thought you said you got eighty percent. That hardly leaves him enough rake-off to be worth the hassle."

The kid looked at me blankly. "Yeah. Like, we cut it, uh, eighty-eighty-twenty-fifty, something like that. So he still end up with like half, you know what I'm saying?"

"I'm guessing you weren't a starter on the math team back when you were in high school," I said.

He blinked. "The *what*?"

"Sorry. Go on."

Superstar studied my face, trying to figure out if I was making fun of him or not. "Yeah. Well, the key to it, you shoot the place up a little. That's what this dude say to me. Make it look good. Otherwise the insurance company won't pay no claim."

"Okay."

"But I only shoot straight up in the ceiling." He grabbed my arm, and pulled me up the aisle until we were standing in front of the register. "Yo, check it out." He pointed at the ceiling.

Sure enough, there were several tiny round holes in the yellowed acoustical ceiling tiles.

"Okay, so you walk in, then what?"

The kid pantomimed with the gun. "I'm like, 'Yo, bi-yetch, gimme the ka-ching, you know what I'm saying.' Pa-yow! Pa-yow! Pa-show!" He aimed his gun at the ceiling, then made a motion like he was pulling a trigger.

"Then it was this big bang. From the lightning. A'ight? And the lights go out for a second. When the lights go back on, that lady be like . . ." He staggered around making large sweeping movements with his gun, presumably to indicate blood spurting out of Phyllis McClint's neck. "Then she just go, clonk. That lady head hit the floor like a coconut."

"And then?"

"And then, I see you. So after that, you seen what happened. I tried to get Mr. Comb-over there to give me the money, and then Five-Oh be riding up outside."

I stood in front of the register, then sighted from eye level across the room past where the woman lay. As best I could tell, there was no bullet hole in the wall on the other side of the room.

Then I studied the blood spattered around the café, trying to see if there was any pattern to the splashes. When somebody gets shot, blood tends to spray out from the wound, allowing you to see the direction the shot came from. Unfortunately there was so much blood that I couldn't make out anything in particular. She must have spun around before she fell. Human blood is under about as much pressure as your standard garden hose. As a result the right kind of wound can project blood as much as ten feet through the air. Phyllis McClint may have set new distance records: her blood was everywhere.

Bottom line, the kid's whole story sounded like nonsense. Most likely he had fired into the ceiling several times with the intention of scaring everybody. But then the lights had gone out. Phyllis McClint had jumped up hoping to flee out the door in the darkness and confusion. Sadly for her, the lights came back on immediately and Superstar, seeing a figure charging toward him, had shot her. Why he was so adamant he hadn't done it, I couldn't figure. Hey, maybe the guy didn't even remember doing it. Maybe he'd blacked it out or something. Or, more likely, it was an idiotic criminal's appropriately idiotic attempt to deny something that any fool could see he had done.

But then, this *was* a guy who thought you could add eighty and eighty and twenty and fifty and end up with a hundred.

"How many shots you fire?"

The kid shrugged. "I don't know. Like, three. Yeah. Three."

"Okay," I said. "So that's your story and you're sticking to it."

The kid nodded. "Three."

"We got a lot of work to do," I said.

Superstar turned and peeped through the blinds. "Yo! Check this out. They got one of them TV trucks out there. Shi-yeeeett, I'ma be on TV!"

He walked down the aisle, looking at everybody in the restaurant in turn, and finally grabbed the yuppie woman. Her husband Patrick had called her Connie. He grabbed her wrist, yanked her out of the booth, wrapped one arm around her neck, put the gun to her temple, and hustled her to the front door, which he pulled open.

"Y'all back off!" he screamed. "Y'all back off or I'ma cap *all* these peoples."

Then he closed the door, came back inside, and patted the woman on her fanny. "You gone look good on the TV, baby."

She gave him a withering look but didn't say anything.

"Go on, baby," the kid said. "Sit down with pretty boy again. But if you need a real man, I'm here for you." He grabbed his crotch, gave it a tasteful squeeze, and did a couple of dry-humping rap-star dance moves.

As Connie was sitting down, the phone by the register rang.

"You want me to answer it?" the waitress said.

But the kid had already picked it up. "Blind Pig, Superstar speaking, how may I help you?" he said brightly.

It was odd, but his mood had changed radically in the last five minutes, going from dark to almost laughably cheery. "Yeah, yeah. That's right. I got hostages, yeah. Uh-huh, and I gots a bomb, too. Two of them. Wired to the front and back doors. Y'all fools try to bust in get all SWAT on my ass, you gone be hosing these people off the street."

He paused, listening.

"You damn right I got demands," he said finally. "I want, uh, a helicopter. And a billion dollars, cash money. Billion, Jack! With a B. And I want to be on *Entertainment Tonight*. Yeeeeeah. 'Cause I do a little bit of vocal stylings, you know what I'm saying? Slamming the mike, you know that's right. No. No. Nah, home boy, *you* listen to this." He held the receiver at arm's length, then banged it down in the cradle.

The bodybuilder in the front booth laughed loudly.

Superstar, who seemed to have been very proud of his performance, stiffened. He walked over to the booth and pointed his pistol in the big man's face. "You got a joke you want to share with the class, dog?" he asked.

"I don't know what's better," the bodybuilder said derisively. "The billion dollars or the thing about *Entertainment Tonight*." He had the same hillbilly-sounding accent as Loretta Lynn, pure Cabbagetown.

"You dissing me? Huh?" the kid said. "You looking to get a cap in your ass?"

The bodybuilder looked unconcerned. "If I was you," he said, "I'd drag that dead chick out the front door, let the cops know you ain't fooling around. Or either shoot somebody else."

"Oh yeah? Maybe I'ma shoot *you*."

"You could do that. But see then—"

The bodybuilder was interrupted. It was the guy with the outrageous gold suit, the guy who had been praying. "For the love of Gawd," the man said, pointing his finger at the bodybuilder, "shut your mouth before he kills somebody else."

The bodybuilder looked at him coolly. "You want a piece of me, dude? Huh?"

"We're all going to die!"

The bodybuilder looked at the man in the gold suit. "Hey, bite me, Royce."

The man with the gold suit was shaking with anger as he pointed at the bodybuilder. "You've brought ruination upon us. You've brought ruination and death upon this entire community. I'm laying this foul murder at your feet just as surely as if you had pulled the trigger-uh!" If I hadn't been in doubt before, the churchy lilt to his voice made it a deadlock certainty that he was a preacher somewhere on the Pentecostal end of the spectrum.

The bodybuilder stood, sticking out his chest. "Yeah? You gonna do something about it or you gonna stand there flapping your lips same as always?"

The kid started pacing up and down, his cheerful mood suddenly evaporating. He seemed to have lost control of the situation.

"I lay down a curse upon you!" yelled the guy with the gold suit, his finger still pointed Solomonically at the bodybuilder. "I call down from heaven all the angels of judgment, in the holy name of Gawd-uh, such that the very—"

Bang!

The guy with the gold suit shut up in midsentence. Superstar had pulled the trigger of his gun, and the noise was so loud it made my ears ring. The ejected cartridge hit the ground and bounced around on the linoleum. I could see it, but I couldn't hear it.

"Shut up! Shut up! Shut up!"

The aftereffects of the gun going off made it seem like Superstar was yelling from down at the end of a very long corridor. Everyone was looking around, trying to see who had been shot. But it was with some relief we all realized the kid had only blasted a hole in the wall.

The phone began to ring. Superstar looked at it, but didn't pick it up. It rang and rang.

"Tell you what, Superstar," I said quietly. Or maybe I was shouting. With the sound of the gun still reverberating in my ears, it was hard to tell.

"Maybe you ought to answer the phone. The cops are going to think you shot somebody."

"Say," the grill man said plaintively. "What about me? My bladder's killing me."

CHAPTER 5

WHILE SUPERSTAR ENGAGED in a brief shouting match with the negotiator on the phone, I eased into the booth where Esther and I had been sitting, and laboriously wrote down a bunch of notes on my legal pad, part of my overall strategy to make every interview eat up as much of the night as possible.

"You really a writer, lady?" Superstar had been pacing nervously around the room after slamming down the phone again. Now he was paused at our table.

"Indeed I am," Esther Nixon said.

"You wrote anything I would of read?"

"When was the last time you read a book?"

The kid thought about it solemnly. "Like, third grade?"

"Then I think you've answered your own question, haven't you?"

"Yeah," the kid pursued, "but I mean are you like famous or something?"

"Let's say, modestly well known. Known to the cognoscenti. Known to the—"

"Lemme put it another way. How many books you done wrote?"

"Upwards of seventy-five, but fewer than one hundred. One hardly keeps count after a certain point."

The kid cleared his throat. " 'Cause, you know, I got like some ideas. For a book."

"Oh, *really*?" Esther batted her eyes and pretended to be fascinated.

"You know, like after this is over, maybe we could get together and like get it wrote down?"

"A fascinating thought, young man. But as we have an opportunity lying right before us, why not embark this very moment. Speak, young man. Your idea—*speak*!"

Superstar ran his tongue around inside his mouth. "Uh. Okay. Okay. Check this out. There's this dude. He's like a karate master and all this shit . . ."

"No profanity, please, young man!"

The kid eyed her uneasily for a moment. "Okay, so there's this karate master dude," he said eventually. "He's about my age you know, and there's these Russian terrorists? And they got this nuke-yu-ler bomb, see, that they done stole from—"

She held up her hand. "Stop! No! No, no, no, *no*!" She stared off into the distance. "No, I'm afraid that's no good. Karate masters are for television. I write books. Besides, a hero should be an underdog. No karate masters. Start over."

The kid looked chastened. "Oh. I didn't know it was no *rules* to writing a book."

"Oh, my dear boy, yes." Esther laughed condescendingly. "But let's not call them rules. Let's call them principles."

"So tell 'em to me."

"Well, first one must decide precisely what one is writing. A mystery? Science fiction? Romance? A thriller? Each has an entirely different set of principles."

"Oh." This seemed to be a stumper for the kid, a vastly disappointing brick wall.

"Besides, one cannot proceed inductively. One must learn these principles by example. I could recite them all to you, but it would do you no good. One must see them in action. Shall I demonstrate?"

The kid seemed to have lost her somewhere around the word *inductively*. He shrugged.

"Very well. Give me an idea—something original, please. No Russian mafiosi, no karate masters. And I shall work out the story right here."

The kid licked his lips. "Shoot, now you putting me on the spot."

"Indeed. Now you're beginning to see the writer's predicament. One is perpetually on the spot." She waited. "Very well. I shall demonstrate. While you stand here, I shall develop a story. Would you like a mystery? A thriller? What, romance?"

"Not romance."

"Very well. A thriller. A special kind of thriller called a caper. Capers don't sell anymore, unfortunately. But that doesn't matter as this is merely a demonstration."

"A caper? Like a scam?"

"Like a scam, yes, or a robbery. Here is how a caper works. The hero is introduced. He must be a small-time criminal or a hapless loser. Out of respect for you, let us start with a hapless loser. What should we name him?"

Apparently the insult went over the kid's head. His brow furrowed for a moment. "Jim."

"Jim? Seems a bit mundane, don't you think?"

The kid pushed out his lower lip a little, digging in his heels. "I said *Jim*."

Esther shrugged. "Jim. Very well. Jim it is. Now Jim has a problem. He's been out of work for some time now. He's broke. There's been . . . let's say he took a fall while working as a construction worker. He initiated a lawsuit to recover workman's compensation, the lawsuit has dragged on, and therefore in order to seal his claim, he's been having to pretend that he has a bad back and can't work, despite being in perfect health. Because of his lawsuit, this once-active young man has given up sports and affected a limp. He doesn't lift anything heavy, doesn't do yard work. He's very determined, you see, to win this lawsuit. Which shows signs, incidentally, of dragging on ad infinitum.

"Now, in order to alleviate the boredom of his sedentary life, he has taken to reading. He reads prodigiously. Books he buys from used book sales, of course, because he doesn't have much money. One day he finds an inscription in the margin of an ancient, yellowed paperback book which says, 'Help me. I'm being held prisoner! Three-fourteen Knight Street. David Hicks!' "

The kid interrupted. "Who's David Hicks?"

Esther smiled tightly. "My dear boy. Principle one. Make them wait. I don't know who David Hicks is any more than you do. We shall have to wait to find out."

"Then how . . ."

"That, my boy, is why the reader continues to read. Because she wants to find out who David Hicks is. If she could find out on the first page, there would be no mystery, no motive power to the story."

"Oh. I see. Damn, this shit *complicated*!"

"Profanity! I shall not continue if you insist on speaking that way."

"Sorry."

"Yes." Esther pushed her nubbly plastic cup across the table to the boy. "Would you be a dear and get me some more tea? I can't think when my mouth is dry."

The kid sighed loudly, but then dutifully trotted over to the counter, poured some tea, came back, set it on the table.

"On a whim," Esther said, "Jim drives his old car over to Knight Street. And guess what he finds? Knight Street is in a subdivision which was built, let us say, in the 1950s. Now, sadly, it is somewhat gone to seed. As he drives down the road he comes the end of the 200 block and to his surprise a huge concrete wall rises up in front of him. He gets out of his car, limps around the barrier, and finds that the 300 block of Knight Street is gone. It has been replaced by a massive ribbon of concrete—Interstate Highway 75, sixteen lanes of traffic, one of the largest highways in the world."

"Hey, dude, that's kind of creepy. But what about this David Hicks?"

"Meanwhile," Esther said, acting annoyed at the interruption. "*Mean*while, we find out that someone is following Jim. A woman in a van with deeply tinted windows. She is taking photographs of him. She is tracking him as though he were a deer in the forest, and she, a cat-footed hunter."

"Whoa." The kid waited, but Esther didn't speak. "Yo, give it up, dude. What happens next?"

Esther looked at me. I had long since quit writing notes in my legal pad. "That's all for now," she said. "Sunny needs to conduct her next interview. Otherwise we shall never get out of here."

"Hold up, dog! I gots to find out what happen next."

"Later. Sunny! Time for your next interview."

I stood and crooked my finger at the next witness.

The man in a shiny gold suit sat on the box in the store room, his smooth-skinned face resting on one hand, tears running down his face. His sandy hair was swept back in a modified pompadour and although he wasn't much overweight, there was a soft jowliness about his face.

"What was that between you and the weightlifter?" I said, when he finally seemed to have composed himself.

"His name's Derl," the man said. "Him and that gal he's sitting with, they're drug dealers. Pushers."

"I see."

"There didn't use to be any drugs in this community. Now they're everywhere. It's all going to pot. Cabbagetown wasn't never no Buckhead. But it was a good community. Good place to raise children. Folks worked hard. Now? Only people got work is the drug pushers."

"What's your name, sir?" I said.

The man looked up suddenly, as though he only just then remembered where he was. "I'm Royce Garrick.

Reverend Royce Garrick. I'm the preacher over to the Memorial Drive Fire Baptized Holiness Church."

"Sunny Childs."

He shook my hand. "I can't believe it. Phyllis is dead."

"Was she a friend?"

"Everybody in Cabbagetown knew Phyllis."

"I'm sorry."

"Praise Gawd, she lived a full life."

I nodded. "Did you see it?"

"See what?"

"See her get shot."

Royce Garrick frowned, looked at the stained floor. "I don't know," he said finally.

"What do you mean, you don't know?"

"Well, I can see him standing up there with the gun. But it was pointed at the ceiling. I remember hearing the gun go off." Reverend Garrick looked slightly embarrassed. "Somewhere in there I kind of, well, truth is, I hid under the table."

"So you saw him with the gun pointed in the air. Do you remember the lightning? And the power going off?"

"Yes ma'am. I believe I do. Phyllis was sitting across the table from me. Then the light went out. Then when they came back on, she was standing up and . . ." He squinted, staring at a rack of jumbo-sized Cheerios boxes. He shook his head. "And that's all I know. I didn't actually see him shoot, I guess that's what I'm saying."

"Because you were under the table."

A deep racking sigh came out of Royce Garrick's mouth. "It's my fault."

"What do you mean?"

"I didn't do nothing to protect her. Nothing at all. I was so busy hiding under the table." The tears started running down his face again. "Oh, Phyllis, Phyllis . . . "

I waited until he'd collected himself. "You were sitting with her? With Phyllis?"

He nodded bleakly.

"What's your relationship to her, if you don't mind my asking."

He looked up sharply. "Relationship?" Then his face relaxed. "Oh, you mean . . ." He smiled tightly. "I thought you were implying—" A brief laugh, almost like a cough. "She was a parishioner of mine."

"You normally eat breakfast at midnight with your parishioners? I'm not trying to pry, you understand, I'm just trying to get a fix on the circumstances."

Royce Garrick got a preachy look on his face. "I'm afraid I couldn't discuss that."

"Meaning what?"

There was a long pause. "I was offering *spiritual* counsel. Beyond that I can't tell you anything."

"Okay. Fair enough."

"The drug dealer. What's his name again?"

"Derl. Spelled D-E-R-L. Derl Pilgrim. His girlfriend is named Shana Marks."

"Do they sell drugs in the restaurant? Or were they just eating?"

"I wouldn't know."

"What kind of drugs do they sell?"

"Crank mostly."

"Crack."

"Not crack. It's a sad testimony that a man of Gawd would know this sort of thing, but to minister effectively in this community . . . well, anyway, not to launch into another sermon, what I said was crank, not crack. Methamphetamines. Crystal meth. Poor man's cocaine." He smiled bitterly. "If it wasn't for people like Derl and Shana, the people like this boy who just killed Phyllis wouldn't be attracted to this community. But all the good people have moved away."

"That's what Loretta Lynn said."

The preacher nodded.

"So how many shots did you hear?"

Royce Garrick looked up at the ceiling thoughtfully as

though he were replaying a tape of the event in his head. "Four."

"You're sure?"

He nodded. "Yes, ma'am. Four. I got a good memory for sound. Three shots, then the lights went out, then one more shot."

"You think it's plausible that somebody else in here shot her?"

There was a long pause.

"What?" I said. "Come on. You seem to be thinking something."

He shrugged. "Derl hates her. He even threatened to kill her once."

My eyes must have widened a little.

"She was head of POCA."

"The neighborhood association."

"Right. Phyllis was a visionary. She recognized that this community only had a future if it got cleaned up. If the drug pushers got forced out, if people got off welfare, if the houses were took care of." He daubed at his eyes again. "She was leading a campaign. They was selling drugs out of an abandoned house over on the other side of Memorial. Phyllis organized a picket, a neighborhood watch sort of thing, regular police patrols. She'd videotape people who came in from the suburbs to buy. She put them out of business. At that location anyway."

"Huh. So this guy Derl, you think he might really kill her if he had the chance?"

The preacher looked off in the distance. "If she let him, he might."

"If *who* let him."

"Shana."

I must have looked puzzled.

"Derl's just muscle," Garrick said. "Shana's had four or five of these here knucklehead boyfriends over the years, every one of them ended up in the penitentiary eventually. Taking the fall for her, one way or other. She's smart. She makes them feel like they're running the show, but they ain't. It's all her."

"So you think he might do it?"

Garrick frowned. "I honestly don't know if he's capable of it or not. My experience, he's mostly mouth."

I nodded. "So other than drug dealers, I assume Phyllis was well liked?"

The minister looked at me with a peculiar expression on his face and cleared his throat. "Phyllis . . . was a difficult person," he said after a brief pause. "Complicated."

"Hard to get along with, you're saying."

"Occasionally."

There seemed to be something bothering him, but I couldn't tell what it was. "What else?" I said finally.

"Oh, it's a hard thing to talk about. Gentrification, they call it. Some of the old Cabbagetown people felt like Phyllis was trying to run out all the regular folks so she could sell off the houses to people like that young couple. The artist fellow and his wife."

"Patrick and Connie?"

"I wouldn't know their names. They don't much mix with us poor peons."

"Did you grow up in Cabbagetown?"

"Yes ma'am."

"You don't have to call me ma'am," I said.

He looked at me dourly. "That's the way I was raised." He scowled. "Not like these kids today." He curled his lip in disgust. "*Superstar!* What is that? He's not the only one. All the kids in the neighborhood are like that now. Tattoos, rings stuck through God only knows what parts of their bodies, talking like colored people, taking nicknames like G-Dog and B-Love and Master Dopey Fool Whatever, their mouths full of foulness and . . ." He sighed loudly. "I've got nothing against the Negroes, African-Americans, black folks, whatever you want to call them, I really don't. But how come young white people got to imitate the worst things about the nig—about the coloreds? I don't get it. There's going to be a Holy Ghost revival, a mighty anointing of the spirit sweeping across this land very, very soon." Royce Garrick's voice rose theatrically. "And I guarantee you when it's over, won't all these children be running around acting like Nigra criminals and musicians."

"Mm-hm," I said.

"Anything else you want to know?"

"Would you object to praying with me a little bit?"

He smiled brightly, took hold of my hand, and squeezed it in a way that seemed not entirely ministerial. "Why sure, sister."

I took my hand back and reached into my purse. "Don't pay any attention to me," I said. "You just pray like the dickens. Nice and loud."

Reverend Royce Garrick looked at me curiously.

I pulled a cell phone out of my purse and speed-dialed a number. "Go on, Reverend," I said. "Pray."

CHAPTER 6

"**B**ARRINGTON," **I SAID** softly, hoping that Superstar wouldn't be able to hear me over the sound of Brother Royce Garrick's droning prayer. "Thank God."

There was a long pause on the other end of the phone. "Sunny? What's wrong?"

Barrington Cherry is my boyfriend. He's with the FBI. He used to be a deputy special agent-in-charge but he quit for a while and then got rehired, so now he's a lowly special agent again. He does undercover narcotics work, and sometimes he's hard to reach. Even at two in the morning. Lately he'd been working an assignment that required a lot of night work, so I was pleasantly surprised when he picked up on the first ring.

I explained as quickly as I could what was going on. It was a strange sensation talking to him. On one hand it was a relief, gave me a slight melting sensation in the gut just to hear his calm, sure voice. But at the same time it was terribly tantalizing, knowing that he was walking around outside, free to come and go as he pleased, while I was cooped up with a heavily armed homicidal idiot.

"I'm going to get down there right away," Barrington said when I was done.

"The cops are doing their job," I said. "The last thing

they'll want is some Fed staring over their shoulders."

"That may be, but—"

"Anyway, there's something I'd like you to do for me."

"Oh?"

"The murder victim here is named Phyllis McClint. You think you could check into her background?"

"Oh, come on," Barrington said. "You don't really think somebody else in there shot her. It's obviously the kid with the gun."

"I know, I know. I'm just trying to be thorough."

"Honestly? This sounds silly to me."

"Humor me, hon. Run her credit bureau, NCIC, the usual stuff."

"Consider yourself humored."

We hung up and then I called 911, got myself patched through to the hostage negotiator, the police major named Drummond, and filled him in on what was happening inside the restaurant.

There was a brief pause after I'd finished talking. "A head shot," the negotiator said finally. "That would be ideal."

"A what?"

"Any chance you could maneuver him to the door somehow? Give our snipers a decent head shot?"

"I thought you were a negotiator."

"Excuse me?"

"I don't know—shooting people in the head, that sounds more like something a SWAT guy would say."

The cop's voice took on an edge. "Young lady, I'm trying to save your bacon. By whatever means are at my disposal."

"Surely you're jumping the gun trying to shoot him right off the bat. At least *talk* to him."

"I have. He's not capable of reason. Didn't you hear him? He wants a billion dollars."

"Major Drummond, this guy wouldn't know the difference between ten thousand bucks and ten billion. He's just farting around. I'm not saying he isn't dangerous, I'm just saying that if you shoot and miss, he's liable to kill somebody else. Even if you hit him, what if the bullet ricochets? You could kill one of us by accident. There's a restaurant full of people in the line of fire."

"So I guess you have some brilliant ideas about how to stop this kid before he kills somebody else, young lady?"

"I'm working on it. But frankly I'm not even sure he's shot *anybody* yet."

I couldn't see his face, of course, but as he spoke I sensed he had a condescending smile plastered across his face. "Why don't you be a good girl and let the police do the police work. Okay? How would that be?"

It wasn't until after I hung up on him that I got to thinking about what I'd just said. Did I actually believe the kid hadn't killed Phyllis McClint? I wasn't sure. It was against all reason, but I honestly wasn't sure.

When I went back into the main part of the café, the grill man was hunched over, a pained expression on his face. "What about *me*, man?"

Superstar glowered at him. "What *about* you?"

"I got that prostrate thing I was telling you about."

"You still going on about that?"

"What, you think my pee is gonna evaporate? Huh?"

"You trying to get me mad? That what you doing?"

The grill man's face had taken on a gray sweaty cast, but you could see he was getting angry. "You idiot kid. I'm gonna wet myself."

"A'ight. Call me a *idiot*? Now you ain't *never* going to no baffroom."

The grill man was shaking slightly. "I got a swole prostrate!" He started yelling it over and over, his voice rising in volume and pitch, and suddenly he was literally jumping up and down. His comb-over had flopped off the side of his head and was waving around like the tail of some greasy rodent.

Superstar picked up a heavy glass saltshaker, tossed it

to Derl. "Here, dude," the kid said. "Go over there and hit Comb-over upside the head."

"Hey . . ." Derl shrugged. "If you say so." He stood up slowly, then walked around the counter, strutting a little, sticking his pecs out, the saltshaker dangling loosely from his hand.

Seeing him coming, the grill man stopped shouting, picked up a spatula and clenched it in his hand like a knife. Derl and the grill man eyed each other for a long moment.

"Don't make me do it, Bobby," Derl said to him.

"All right, all right," the grillman said, pawing at his greasy comb-over. "I'll wait."

Derl faked lazily like he was going to whack the grill man with the saltshaker and the cook flinched. Derl laughed and flung a sprinkling of salt at him.

How much longer? I couldn't help thinking it. *How much longer before things started breaking down and someone else died?* Maybe the police negotiator on the phone was right. Would it be better if they sent a SWAT team to blast the door down and come in shooting.

CHAPTER 7

"YO, SUNNY," SUPERSTAR said when we came out of the storeroom. "You see? I ain't did it."

"Look, I'm still gathering information. Being a detective is painstaking work. It can't be rushed. First you gather the information, then you draw conclusions."

The kid looked at me like I was speaking Serbo-Croatian.

"Okay, fine," I said. "Next I want to talk to Derl."

The big muscle builder looked at me with narrowed eyes. "How come?"

"You were closest to Superstar."

"Superstar? Shoot. Super Dumb-Ass, more like it."

The kid turned and pointed his gun at Derl. "Yo, bi-yetch. Keep talking. Huh? Keep talking."

Derl gave him a jailhouse stare. "You a big talker long as you got that gun, ain't you. Whyn't you put that thing down, you and me go outside, see who's the big dog."

"Guys!" I said. "Quit acting like morons before somebody else gets killed."

The kid and Derl had a long staring contest.

"Come on back here, Derl," I said. "Let's talk."

"You heard the lady, homes," Superstar chimed in. "Get your fat ass back there."

Derl gave him a few seconds more eyeball, then stood up and walked down the aisle toward me, doing a parody of Superstar's limping pimp strut. "Yeeeeeee-ah," Derl said. "Dashright, ladies. I'm Shupahfly, Shupahstah, Shupah-dupah Lady Killah."

"Knock it off," I said.

Derl winked at Connie, the pretty yuppie, who tried unsuccessfully to stifle a grin.

"Connie, for Chrissake, ignore him," her husband hissed.

Derl brushed the side of Connie's face with his pinky finger as he walked by, then broke into a normal stride and followed me into the storeroom.

When I stopped, he kept walking, only stopping once he'd gotten uncomfortably close to me. It was obvious he enjoyed physical intimidation. I'm five feet tall and weigh about a hundred pounds. He easily weighed twice what I do—probably more—and was a good foot taller.

I've studied martial arts for a long time, and one thing I've learned is that most physical conflicts get resolved before the first blow is struck. Derl wasn't looking to actually lay a hand on me. He just wanted me to know that he could if he felt like it. Sometimes a guy like that, you have to head him off at the pass.

I said to him, "My old karate instructor, Kenzo Shimura, once said to me, 'Women talk about the pain of childbirth and I have no doubt that they're sincere. But one does not know the meaning of pain until one has been hit in the testicles.' So what I'm wondering is if that's true."

"Do *what*?" Derl said.

I reached out and grabbed the muscle builder by the crotch. Not squeezing, just holding on firmly enough that he couldn't get away without causing me to clamp down on some fairly sensitive parts of his anatomy.

"Hey . . ." His voice went up a notch.

"What the hell were you doing out there?" I said.

"Let go. Damn, girl! Let go of my—"

"I asked you a question. There's a guy out there with

a gun, and you're trying to see who's the biggest bull in the prison yard. Frankly I don't care if he shoots you, but this kid is unpredictable right now. I'd really prefer he not blow holes in *me* just because *you're* acting like a dipshit."

"Hey, I was just fooling around, girl." The big man's voice was whiny now and a sweat had broken out on his forehead. I squeezed just a hair tighter.

"In the future, don't."

"Let go. Please?"

I gave him a last little squeeze, then shoved him backward. He sat down on a box of toilet paper, pressing his hands into his crotch. Royce Garrick was right: the guy folded up pretty easily once you got past his big mouth.

"Okay, you know why we're here. I want to know if you saw that kid shoot Phyllis."

Derl looked at me resentfully. "Of *course* he shot her."

"That's not what I asked. I asked if you *saw* him shoot her."

Derl rubbed himself a little bit, grimacing. Then a tiny glimmer came into his eye. "Hell, yeah, I saw it." He lifted his hand, pointed his finger at me, thumb poking straight up. "Pow. Shot her right in the by-God head."

"He shot her in the neck."

"Well, he was *aiming* at her head. I guess he missed."

I studied his face. He looked like a four-year-old kid trying to convince you he hadn't snuck the popsicle out of the freezer even though there was purple stuff smeared all over his face. "I think you're lying to me, Derl. I think as soon as the first shot that went off, you were laying on the floor covering your head with your hands."

"I don't give a damn what you think, lady," he mumbled, looking at the floor.

I sat down on a milk crate and watched him for a while.

"So," I said finally. "I understand you didn't much like Phyllis McClint."

"*Nobody* liked Phyllis McClint."

"Is that so?"

"Straight up."

"How come not?"

"You wouldn't understand."

"Why not?"

"You got to be a cabbagehead to understand why every-body hates her so much."

"What's a cabbagehead?"

"Somebody that growed up in Cabbagetown."

"Okay, I'm a smart girl. Explain it to me."

"I can't. It's too complicated."

"Try."

The big man shifted around in his seat. "Look," he said finally. "My mama told me about how it used to be. Thirty, forty, fifty years ago, this area was all white peo-ple. Working people. Even back then, we was different. They called us Cabbageheads, white trash, hillbillies, all that. But then the whites moved out, and the niggers, man, they flat closed in around us. By the time I was born, south of Ponce de Leon Avenue, there wasn't one single white person left. Except us." He laughed bitterly. "You turn on the TV today, you can't help hearing people talk-ing about all the discrimination, all the bad things that happens to black people in America and stuff. Shit. You ain't never seen what it's like to be a minority till you been a white person in a place that's 99 percent niggers. Way things are today, if a white person hates a nigger, he's got to dress it up a little, hide it, you know? Or they throw the book at you. They'll call it a hate crime or discrimination or something, you'll have federal agents and lawyers all over you. But niggers, man, they can do any damn thing they want to white people—*poor* white people anyway—and nobody cares. The niggers hated us. The rich white folks up in Buckhead forgot us. After the cotton mill closed down, there wasn't no jobs. We was all alone down here. Alone, broke, forgotten. So us cab-bageheads, we had to stick together."

He waved his arm around in a large circle. "This place, you drive down here from your ritzy subdivision or wherever you come from, I'm sure y'all are like, man, what a *shitass* place. Crummy old falling-down houses, itty-bitty yards full of weeds, old junk cars parked on the street . . ."

He shook his head. "But this here's my home. These people are *my* people. I may get drunk and get in a fight with some old boy from down the street. Some lady might not like what I do for a living. I might not get along with half the people on the street around here. But I don't care about that. They's *my* people. Somebody come in from the outside, start hassling a cabbagehead, by God, I got their back. Who*ever* it is. That's what it's like being a cabbagehead."

"Okay, fair enough. But what's that got to do with Phyllis?"

He squinted and looked up in the air. "What it is, Phyllis McClint's a traitor."

"I don't follow."

"She set up this POCA thing, the neighborhood association, a few years back. And a lot of people around here thought it was good. POCA, they helped a couple folks get low-interest loans to fix their houses, tried to spruce things up a little, tried getting rid of, uh, certain freelance pharmaceutical salesmen who I ain't gonna mention by name. The whole thing was like, let's help each other out, maybe we can keep this place from going colored for another five, ten years. And most people was okay with all of that.

"But see, Phyllis, she had an agenda behind all that. I don't like her, but I'll tell you this much. She's a smart lady. She seen it all coming."

"Saw what coming?"

"Y'all."

I must have looked puzzled.

"Rich people."

"I'm not rich people."

Derl laughed. "Look around you. Look at them falling-down houses, the old cars, people sitting out on the curb drinking beer out of paper bags, then tell me you ain't rich compared to us."

"So you're talking about gentrification."

He smiled. "It's all about getting paid, baby."

"I'm not sure I understand what you're getting at."

"Take a map of Atlanta. Draw a line right smack dab through the center, left to right. From Ponce de Leon south, this here's a black city. From Ponce north, white. For about thirty, forty years, that line's done been moving north. Every year further and further north. But something funny happened about five, ten years ago. All of a sudden rich white people got tired of driving for an hour to some job in a high-rise building downtown, driving an hour to get back out to the suburbs.

"So what happened? White people started buying up property in working-people-type neighborhoods on the north side of town. But eventually they done ran out of regular old white folks to run off. So what's left? Black neighborhoods. Grant Park, Summerhill, places like that. Well, shoot, pretty soon these white people that's done forgot about Cabbagetown, they're like, *Damnation, there's a white neighborhood down there! Maybe we ought to check it out.*

"Next thing you know some hippie-looking artists or a couple of faggots is moving in next door. Painting, planting petunias, sticking up fences so nobody's dog gonna shit in the yard." Derl shrugged. "That happens once or twice, you're like, hey, ain't that nice, maybe this crummy-ass neighborhood is making a comeback. We done held out against the niggers and won, by God!" He smiled an ugly little smile.

"We survived the cotton mill shutting down. We survived the niggers and the welfare reform and the town falling apart. But then we come to see after the eighth or the tenth or the twelfth house sells out to the yuppies, hey, it ain't the niggers that's the enemy. It's *y'all.*" He pointed his finger at my chest. "The one thing we never thought we'd have to beat is y'all."

"So you're saying Phyllis McClint was accelerating the process."

"Accelerating the process. Man, y'all *do* know how to talk up there, don't you."

"Well, what then?"

"Like I say, it's all about getting paid. Always has been, always will be. All this time we thought the niggers was the enemy, but it turns out them poor sonsabitches is in the same boat as us. Poor white, poor black, don't matter. Poor is poor. Us cabbageheads, we always lost out to big-money people. Bunch of rich folks brung us down here out of the mountains a hundred years ago, and now a bunch of rich folks gonna kick us out again."

"You keep talking around the point. Where does Phyllis McClint fit into this?"

"Phyllis, she been buying up property around here. Secret. On the cheap. Whispering in old men's ears. How they could sell out for twenty-five, thirty thousand bucks, she'd make sure they got in a nice nursing home or something, have a little comfort in their declining years, that type of thing. And then guess what, that same house gets sold to some hippy artist or some faggot for sixty-five or eighty-five thousand dollars. And who's making all the ka-ching? Miss Let's-Save-Cabbagetown."

"Okay, but the question is, is there somebody in this restaurant that would want to kill Phyllis for that?"

Derl fixed his eyes on me for a long moment. "In Cabbagetown, if you cut a man up with a razor, beat up your wife, burn down somebody's house, shoot somebody's dog, hey, shit happens. You get back from the penitentiary, go down to the church, raise some Cain, cry, tell everybody what a pitiful sinner you are, everybody forgives you. Nah, in Cabbagetown there's only one real sin. That's selling out your people."

"So would anybody in this restaurant have wanted to kill her for that?"

He shrugged. "I done told you it was that kid. Superstar."

I drummed my fingers on the side of the milk crate I was sitting on. A large moth fluttered around the bare bulb overhead, throwing creepy shadows around the room.

"I'm given to understand that you threatened to kill Phyllis yourself."

Derl gave me a hard look. "No ma'am."

"I'm also given to understand she ran you and Shana out of a profitable drug sales spot."

"A *what*?"

"Oh, come on, don't tell me you're going to pretend you're not a dealer."

He smirked. "You been listening to Brother Royce, haven't you?"

"I'm not telling you where I'm getting my information."

The smirk didn't go away. "What's the first thing you notice about old Royce? Huh?"

I didn't say anything.

"Him and my older brother Larry come up together. You know what they used to call him back when they was kids?"

"Why should I care?"

"Nose. They called him Nose. You want to know why?"

"I bet you're going to tell me whether I want you to or not."

"Royce Gerrick, they called him Nose, because he could smell poontang a mile away."

I spread my hands apart raised my eyebrows a little. "And?"

"Bet you didn't ask the man of God if he was slicing him off a piece, did you?"

"You're saying he was having an affair with Phyllis?"

"I'm saying she did whatever it took to get things rolling in her direction. I'm saying good old Nose out there is in a position to influence a lot of old retired ladies about what to do with their houses. I'm saying Phyllis McClint would go down on a pissed-off boar hog for fifty cents."

"Let's say that was true. I still don't see the relevance."

"Gimme a break, girl. You asking if anybody here had a motive to kill her. And I'm telling you she chewed up good old Brother Royce and spit him out like a bad piece of meat."

"Meaning what?"

"Meaning she got him to con a bunch of old ladies into selling their houses to her, and once he done it, she dumped him."

"When was that?"

"Last week."

"How do you know that?"

"I'm a cabbagehead, man. Ain't no secrets in Cabbagetown."

"So if she dumped him last week, why were they meeting here in the middle of the night?"

"Beause he's one seriously pussy-whipped man of God."

"So he had motive."

"You keep talking motive, and I keep telling you. I seen the kid shoot her. Seen it plain as day."

I held up my finger, pulled out my cell phone, dialed my boyfriend Barrington's number. "Me again," I said. "You find out anything about Phyllis?"

"Ran her through NCIC. Only one thing on her record."

"Which was."

"Vagrancy."

"Vagrancy?"

"Used to be if you got arrested for prostitution and the case was weak they'd plead it down to vagrancy."

"I see. What about credit?"

"I ran her credit bureau. She had some trouble about five years ago. Slow paying, mostly. Looks like she ran up more bills than she could handle. But for the past few years she's been paying off her cards religiously at the end of every month. There's no car note, so whatever she drives, she paid cash for."

"Thanks, sweetheart."

I had just stuffed the cell phone back in my pocket when Superstar poked his head around the corner. "Y'all done yet?"

My heart was beating hard in my throat. He'd almost caught me. I tried to smile. "As a matter of fact . . ."

CHAPTER 8

I T'S HARD TO explain the way time passes when somebody has a gun trained on you. It's like every second sinks a hook in your flesh, and you have to tear it out just to move on to the next second. And just when a few seconds go by in sequence without you thinking of dying, something pops up that reminds you that this might be it for you. For me, the thing that kept jumping out was Phyllis McClint herself, lying in a heap in the middle of the aisle.

Death is supposed to be solemn. But what strikes you about looking at a person who's been murdered is not just how sad and horrifying it is, but how strangely degrading—even embarrassing—it seems. Phyllis McClint's skirt had ridden up as she fell, exposing a little cellulite on one thigh and a few dark hairs she'd missed when shaving her legs. Her slip, which poked out from under her skirt, was stained pink with blood in a way that reminded me more of that ultimate junior high school trauma, the menstrual accident, than it did anything deeply tragic. Her feet were pigeon-toed. Her mouth lolled open, exposing her tongue. Her makeup was smeared. She stared up in the air, slightly cross-eyed, giving her the expression of a retarded person.

"For godsake, Superstar," I said quietly as Derl walked back to his seat, "you've got to do something about that woman's body. It's not right to just leave her laying there."

The kid glanced at her briefly, as though he could barely even look at her.

"Y'all two old men," he said, turning to the table where the four old folks sat. "Y'all feel up to a little back labor?"

"I can hold up my end of things, I reckon," one of the old guys said.

"Make you a deal. If you and Grandpappy here drag this lady outside, I'll let y'all go."

"I ain't going without my wife," the old guy said.

Superstar shrugged. "Don't make no difference to me. Take the old ladies with you."

"Reckon that's okay," the old man said. The two men looked almost identical in the face, hollow-cheeked and weathered—but one of them had hair that had once probably been carrot red, though now it was just a grizzled ginger.

"What about *me*?" the grill man said. "Them two old farts is healthy as horses. I got a bad prostate, now I'm fixing to wet my pants."

"If you don't shut up . . ." Superstar said.

The grill man looked away sullenly muttered something.

"Hold on, hold on," I said. "Does anybody have a camera?"

"What?" the kid said.

"A camera. If you really didn't do this, then I trust you'd want photographs taken to document the crime scene. They'd help the forensics people prove you didn't do it."

I watched the boy's face to see how he reacted. I didn't expect anybody to have a camera. It was more just to get a reaction out of the kid. Something seemed to be dawning inside his thick skull, but I couldn't tell what it was. "How would they do that?"

"Lots of ways. Blood spatter analysis, body position, wound direction. It's all science." I said it all in a confident, breezy tone, still watching for a reaction.

The kid poked his tongue out the corner of his mouth and looked down at the dead woman for a while. "Good thinking, dude," he said finally. Then he looked around the room. "Huh? People? Huh? Anybody got a camera?"

The yuppie woman, Connie, held up a camera, a new Polaroid.

"For chrissake Connie," her husband said. "That camera cost seventy-five bucks. Now we'll never get it back."

Connie smiled brightly at him. "So get a job, Patrick. Then you can buy a new one."

I took the camera and walked around the dead woman, taking pictures. I took wide shots from three or four angles, then close-ups of Phyllis's face, of the horrible wound in her neck, of her hands, of her feet. When I was done I had a stack of Polaroids on the counter.

I gave the camera back to Connie, then turned to the two old men. "You need any help, sir?" I said to the old men.

"I believe we'll be all right," the red-haired old guy said.

The two old men motioned for their wives to stand. They were all tough-looking old people, but worn hard by work and poverty and age. One of the women had swollen ankles and could barely hobble, even with the assistance of a cane. The other one walked okay, but was bent over nearly double from some kind of back problem. They walked slowly, painfully toward the door.

Behind them the two old men picked up the dead woman's feet and began dragging her toward the door. It seemed endless, their sad procession. I wanted to look away, but I couldn't: the two bent-over old women, the two grim old men in overalls and ancient brogans. As they dragged her toward the door, Phyllis's skirt began riding higher and higher, until finally her panties were showing. The old man with ginger hair started fumbling with her skirt, trying to keep her from being exposed, but it only served to slow him down. Behind them they left a long red swath of blood on the scarred, murky brown linoleum.

The procession staggered on and on and on and on, like some endless parade from hell.

When they finally got the door open I caught a glimpse of men in black uniforms running forward to shield the old people and pick up the body.

The kid grabbed me by the throat then, the gun laid up against my face, and pulled me to the door.

"Get back!" he screamed out at the oncoming police. "Get back, all y'all sonsabitches, or everybody in here's dead meat!"

The SWAT guys crept backwards toward the ring of cop cars, then the kid hauled me back inside and slammed the door.

There was a long silence, then the kid let go of me, his hand gradually relaxing until it was gentle as a feather.

I looked over at the table where the two yuppies sat and saw that Patrick had the camera clenched in his hands so hard that his knuckles were white, and tears were running silently down his face.

CHAPTER 9

"Y'ALL GOT ANY tools in here?" Superstar yelled at Loretta Lynn.

"What kind of tools?"

"Tools! Tools!" The kid was looking nervous, suddenly, almost frantic. I guess seeing all those SWAT guys with their helmets and body armor and submachine guns had thrown a scare into him.

"There's a toolbox under the counter." Loretta Lynn pointed.

The kid vaulted over the counter, pulled out a military surplus steel ammunition case, opened it, rummaged around inside and came out with a hammer and a rust-speckled paper bag of nails.

"What about some wood? Boards, plywood, something like that."

"They's a few pieces of four-by-eights in the storeroom," the grill man said. "Plywood."

"Anybody in here do any carpentry?"

There was a brief moment of silence, then Patrick held up his hand hesitantly. "I'm kind of fixing up our place over on Gaskill Street," he said. "I'm doing a little framing, some drywall, molding, that sort of thing. Now if you're looking for finish carpentry, you might—"

Superstar interrupted him. "Hey! Did I axe for your life story? No. I did not. Go in the storeroom, get the plywood out, and then I want you to nail the front and back doors shut. The front window, too. Got it?"

Patrick nodded.

"I can help," I said. "Get it done quicker."

"Most girls I know can't nail worth nothing."

"I'm not most girls."

"Excuse *me*!" Superstar waggled his head then shrugged. "Shoot, baby, go ahead. You want to nail, go nail."

He took a second hammer out of the toolbox, tossed it on the counter.

I helped Patrick drag the plywood out. He took two pieces up front and I took one back to the back door. He had nailed the front door and the front window shut before I even finished with the back door. Based on the results, I had exaggerated my skills with a hammer: most of the nails were bent, and I indulged in a little creative cursing as I went.

It only took about ten minutes, but every fall of the hammer was ominous and jarring, every flat smack of steel driving us deeper into the dark place we had entered. By the time we were done it looked as though there would be no way out, at least not without pry bars or explosives.

"Who you gonna talk to now, Sunny?" the kid said to me.

I walked casually to the toolbox to return the hammer. As I did so, I scanned the jumble of tools, looking for a weapon. An Exacto knife, an awl—anything I could use as a weapon if I got caught in a corner. But there was nothing sharp in the toolbox, and I knew that if I didn't return the hammer, the kid would notice.

There was, however, a pry bar, the short kind made of a ribbon of steel with a nail hook at the end. In the right circumstances, you could kill somebody with it. I hesitated and glanced up at Superstar. He was looking at me uninterestedly.

"Looks good, huh?" I waved at the front window.

Superstar glanced at it without interest. That gave me my chance. I palmed the pry bar, slid it up my sleeve, then dropped it from there into my coat pocket. My heart was racing. I had no doubt the kid would beat me—or worse—if he saw what I was doing. Glancing back to me, the kid said, "Yo, girl, I axed who you gonna talk to next."

I turned and did my best to amble back to my chair, but my legs were so weak I could hardly walk.

"I guess I'll interview the grill guy. What's his name?"

"Bobby," Loretta Lynn said.

I looked around the restaurant but the grill man was nowhere to be seen.

"Bobby?" I called. "Hey, Bobby?"

"He probably snuck back to the bathroom in all the excitement," Loretta Lynn said.

Superstar's eyes clouded. "I told him to . . ." He broke off and stalked rapidly back to the back of the restaurant. The toilets were tucked into an L-shaped nook that you couldn't see from the front. The kid turned the corner and banged on the door with his fist. "Yo, Comb-over! Get out here!"

There was no answer, so Superstar started kicking the door. "Yo! Yo!"

Nobody answered.

"Hey!" Superstar kicked the door several more times, working himself into a rage. "Hey!"

"I'm telling you—what's your name? Bobby? I'm telling you, Bobby, you don't get out in five seconds, I'ma mess you up. Five, four, three, two . . ."

A small string of spit flew out of Superstar's mouth as he rared back and kicked the flimsy door one last time. The lock gave way and the door bounced open.

I peered past him into the tiny bathroom. It was empty. Urinal full of cigarette butts, ancient toilet, paper towel dispenser. Otherwise nothing. No doors, no windows, no way out.

"God*dammit*!" Superstar backed out, flung open the door to the women's bathroom, pointed his gun into the room. The cramped little cell was also empty.

But unlike the men's room, it had a small window. And that window was wide open, a frigid draft flowing into the café.

"So much for Bobby, huh?"

"Man!" Superstar said, looking angry but also a little sheepish. "I *knew* he didn't need to go to no baffroom. Big fat *liar!*" Superstar seemed personally offended, as though the guy were some kind of deviant for wanting to escape from being a hostage.

I studied the window. It was about a foot high and two feet wide, six feet off the ground. I had a hard time seeing the beefy old cook climbing through there. But it was obvious that that was what had happened. He must have stood on the plumbing pipe above the toilet and slid out headfirst. Apparently desperation and fear could drive a large peg through an awful small hole.

Superstar ran back into the main part of the café, then pointed at Patrick. "Yo. Pretty boy. Take that hammer over there and nail the ladies' room door shut."

After Patrick had finished with the door, the phone next to the register rang, and Superstar snatched up the receiver.

"Yo, *what*?" he said angrily.

There was a brief pause. I assumed it was Drummond, the hostage negotiator talking on the other end.

"Y'all must think I'm some kind of dumb-ass," he said. "You think I ain't watched one of them movies? The negotiator out there trying to engage your trust? 'Hey, just call me John, I'm a man of my word,' all that? Nah, nah, nah, Major. We done had this conversation. I want me a chopper. Out on the street. Full tank of gas. I want me a billion dollars. Unmarked bills. In a suitcase. In the chopper. I done told you all of this before, you already got *one* dead lady lying in the road. How long you plan on trying to stall me? Huh? Huh? Okay then."

Superstar looked around the café. "What time it is?"

"Two-fifteen," I said.

"A'aight," Superstar said into the phone. "If you ain't got my chopper and my money by five-fifteen this morning, I'm gonna waste everybody." There was a brief pause. "Oh, and don't forget, I want to be on *Entertainment Tonight,* too."

He slammed down the phone, glowered around the room. "What? Y'all think I'm joking? Three hours. Either Sunny Childs gonna solve how it wasn't me done this murder and she gonna do that affidavit thing to the cops, or else they gonna give me a billion dollars. That or everybody in here gonna die. *Everybody gonna die!*"

He stalked around the café looking people in the eye, bending down in front of Patrick, then Connie, then Derl and Shana. "Three hours, bay-bee!" he would say to each in turn. "Three hours, do or die."

When he got back to the table where Esther Nixon was sitting he said, "Oh, hey, I forgot. What happen next? I want to find out who this David Hicks dude is."

CHAPTER 10

VERYBODY IN THE café was listening as Esther continued with the story she had started telling earlier.

"Principle Two, you see, young man, is this: the hero or heroine must always be in a predicament."

"A predicament."

"*Exactamente.* Watch this. Our hero, Jim, returns home from the bookstore to find a message from his lawyer. This lawsuit that he's engaged in has finally been scheduled for trial. Which means that he only has to carry on his bad back charade for another six weeks. Of course he's heavily invested in this lawsuit by now. He's borrowed some money to support himself—because of course he hasn't been working—and so he's in a hole and desperately needs to win the case in order to get himself squared away financially. So he's very excited.

"Still, of course, he has nothing but time on his hands, and so he decides to see if there are any David Hickses in the phone book. As it happens, there are three. He drives to each of their houses in turn. The first two he rules out as being connected to the inscription in the book: they were both too young and neither had ever lived on Knight Street.

"So he gets to the third guy and he's disappointed. Another young guy. But he talks to him anyway, asks if he knows anybody who has the same name who might have been alive in the early 1950s. Well, yes, the young man says. I was named after my uncle. Oh, well, where is he? He's dead. He disappeared back in 1954. Body never found, that sort of thing, when he was twelve years old."

Superstar butted in. "Hey, what about that female that was driving around after this dude. In the van? You remember that?"

"Funny you should mention her," Esther said. "As he drives away from the curb at David Hicks Number Three's house, she's watching him. She picks up her cell phone and calls someone."

The kid kept watching her. "Well?" he said finally. "Who'd she call?"

Esther looked at him and blinked several times. "Don't you think it's time Sunny did another interview?" she said sharply.

The kid sighed. He seemed torn. Finally he turned to me and said, "Okay, what's next?"

I pointed at Shana, the alleged drug queenpin of Cabbagetown. "Her."

Shana was five foot six or seven and her hair wasn't dyed or sprayed or teased, but hung limply off her head. No big hair here. Other than a great smear of eyeliner, she wore no makeup. Her skin was large-pored and sallow. She was bony and teatless, with large prominent veins in her arms and hipbones protruding from the tops of her jeans. She was not good-looking by any conventional measure. And yet there was something about her, a churlish, vital gleam in her eyes that I felt certain men would find attractive. When she sat motionless, she was nearly invisible; but as soon as she began to move—it was hard to put your finger on the exact quality—but there was something charismatic about her. She was graceful, for one thing. But more than that, there was something about her that sucked your eyes toward her when she moved.

I noticed Patrick watching her, too, an odd hunger in his eyes. His wife, however, watched Patrick's face, and her eyes clouded with anger.

"What's your game, girlfriend?" Shana said once she'd walked into the room.

"Sit down," I said sharply. I had decided the only way to play her was to go straight at her.

She eyed me with apparent amusement, then sprawled her lanky body down on the toilet paper box in the windowless storeroom

"You working a angle here, Sunny. Any fool can see that."

"Be that as it may . . ." I drummed my fingers on the shelf next to me, where there were about fifty cans of fruit cocktail lined up. "I understand your boyfriend threatened Phyllis once. Said he was going to kill her."

Shana looked at me with a half smile on her face and waggled her head slightly. Her pink tongue moved slowly across her lower lip, then disappeared. "So."

"Gives him a motive, doesn't it?"

Shana laughed loudly. "Honey, it's a red letter day if Derl makes it to breakfast without saying he's gonna kill somebody."

"Doesn't mean he didn't do it."

"I bet there ain't ten people in Cabbagetown he ain't said he was gonna kill over the years. But you know what? He ain't killed a one of them yet. And he ain't gonna."

"Why not?"

" 'Cause he's all talk and no action. Derl ain't nothing but a mama's boy."

I thought about it, and from what I'd seen she was right.

"Anyway, let me get this straight," Shana said. "You're saying that the lights go off and somebody has the presence of mind to go, 'Well, doggone, I'd sure like to kill her and now looks like a handy moment.' Then they pull out a gun, they shoot her once, make a perfect shot while the lights are still out, hide the gun while the lights are out, then sit there innocent as pie."

"I know, I know," I said. "It sounds a little improbable."

"Improbable? I don't know about that. Sounds plain old stupid to me."

I flushed. Shana may have been a dope-dealing scumbag, but she had a talent for making me feel inadequate.

"Look," I said, "I'm just trying to slow things down, give this Superstar character time to make a mistake."

"Then what? You gonna bash his head in with that pry bar you done stole out the toolbox?"

I flushed again. "Just keeping my options open. Anyway the main thing is, the more time I take, the more chance I give this guy to cool down."

Shana laughed derisively. "Don't be stupid."

"What do you mean?"

"What, you didn't notice? He's hyped up on crank, snorts it every fifteen minutes."

"You sell it to him?"

Shana studied my face for a long moment. She had blue eyes so pale they looked almost white from some angles. "You sound like a cop, you know that?"

"Well, I'm not."

"Anyway, reason I mention it, time ain't on our side, not with this guy wacked out on crank. The later it gets, the crazier he's gonna get."

I thought about it for a while. "I don't see that changing anything. His stash will eventually run out, right? Then he'll crash and fall asleep or something."

"You obviously ain't seen his stash."

"You saw it?"

"He was trying to sneak a toot without nobody seeing him. But I seen him pull out his bindle."

"How much did he have?"

"Let's put it this way, he's carrying distribution weight." Meaning he was carrying enough to get convicted of possessing the drugs with an intent to distribute.

"So he's not going to run out of crank tonight?"

"Not this *week*."

I thought about it for a moment. Presumably Shana had the professional eye to gauge how long his stash would hold out.

"You mentioned presence of mind a few moments ago," I said. "Would *you* have the presence of mind to kill Phyllis and ditch the weapon, given the chance?"

"I might. But what would be the motive for that?"

"Phyllis used her organization, COPA, to shut down your crack house."

"I never had no crack house. But let's just say I was in the recreational pharmaceuticals industry—which I ain't admitting to—I'd figure that type of thing was just the cost of doing bidness. Plus which, killing somebody, especially a citizen, all that's gonna do is bring down the law on you. Nah, me, I'd probably just rent me another squat over on the other side of Memorial Drive, get right back to work."

"But suppose you could do it and get away with it."

"What would be the point?"

"A warning to other people."

Shana looked disgusted. "Honey, look around you. The yuppies is moving in. They done it in Grant Park, all these other places, now they doing it in Cabbagetown. The one thing you can be sure of about yuppies, they ain't gonna let nobody sell dope in their neighborhood. They'll get all organized, march around, bitch to the cops, the whole nine. Shoot, I could murder off everybody in the dadgum neighborhood, five minutes later I'd be in jail and it'd be wall-to-wall BMWs, bunch of rich people trying to buy up cut-rate real estate. So why bother? There's plenty of places left."

"It might scare enough people to buy you another six months. From what I know about most drug dealers, six months is a lifetime."

"Yeah, that's true. Most folks got a short-term mentality. Drug dealers included. But not me. I got a plan."

"Which is what?"

Shana shrugged, gave me a mysterious smile. "I'm looking into various things. *Legit* things."

I figured I'd gone about as far with this line of attack as I could, so I decided to change the subject. "Okay, Shana. Let's get back to the matter at hand. Tell me what you know about Phyllis."

"What I *know* about her?"

"General impressions."

"She's a pushy, smart-mouth, snooty know-it-all. I ain't glad she's dead, but I ain't sorry either."

"I heard she was using POCA as a front to help her make money in real estate."

Shana looked away from me and shrugged again. "Everybody got to get paid somehow."

"So it wouldn't bother you if she were doing that?"

"Why would it bother *me*? I done told you, the writing's on the wall. The yuppies are coming. Another five years, all us redneck white trash hillbillies gonna be history. Might as well make a little ka-ching on the way out."

"Anybody she might have run afoul of that way?"

Shana sighed. "If I was you, and I was taking this idea seriously—which I most definitely ain't—that somebody in here besides this moron done shot her, where I'd look is in the jealous boyfriend department."

"Royce Garrick."

"Him or any other man in the joint."

"Meaning what?"

"If there's a man in this place that she ain't spread her legs for, it ain't 'cause she didn't try."

"Bobby, the cook?"

"Hey, you never know."

"Derl?"

"Oh, I *know* she's fooled around with Derl. But like I say, even if he was mad at her, he's too soft to have did anything about it."

"Who's the fat guy up front by himself. The one who looks a little . . ."

"The retard? That's Benny. Okay, you could probably

rule him out. He ain't got the brains of a gnat. Wouldn't be nothing in it for her to fool around with him."

"Patrick?"

"That pretty-looking boy? He *is* kind of cute, ain't he? Wouldn't object to giving him a test drive myself. And if I've thought about it, you *know* Phyllis has." She flashed me a randy smile. One of her eye teeth was missing.

"One last question. What exactly did you see when Superstar came in?"

Her smile faded. "Nothing."

"What, you weren't looking?"

"I had my back to it."

"You didn't hear him yell, 'This is a stick-up' or whatever he said? You didn't turn around to look?"

"I heard it."

"So? What then?"

Her face relaxed and she suddenly seemed to be absolutely without character. "See this?" she said. "When the heat comes down, I just turn invisible."

I stared at her. It was a fascinating transformation, from a lively bright woman to someone who could just as well have been zoned out on codeine.

Suddenly the mask dropped away. "That's all I done, just slid down in the seat, pretended I wasn't there. Didn't look, didn't talk, didn't do nothing."

"So you're facing the rear of the restaurant. If somebody in the back of the restaurant had fired a gun, you would have seen it. Even in the dark, you'd have seen a flash, right?"

Shana curled her upper lip slightly. "Maybe."

"But you didn't see it."

"Nope."

"So I take it you think Superstar shot her?"

"Superstar?" She scowled at me. "Stop calling him that. It's annoying me."

"What should I call him then?"

"On the street they call him 'L' or Loser. His real name's Keith. Keith Trice."

"How do you know that? Is he from Cabbagetown?"

"Nah. He's just a alley dog."

"Alley dog?"

"That's what we call homeless people around here. But he, uh, he might have been a client once or twice. Hypothetically speaking, of course. See, I'm the type gal if I was a drug dealer, I'd make a point of knowing my clientele. Who they was, where they lived, that type thing. Keeps the snitches and the rats in line."

"Keith Trice?" I pulled out my cell phone. "I don't suppose you know his Social Security number, huh?"

She looked at my cell phone and raised her eyebrows slightly. "You just full of tricks ain't you?"

I spoke into the phone. "Barrington, hi, me again. Got another name for you to run through NCIC."

CHAPTER 11

HE PHONE BY the register rang and Keith Trice picked it up with his usual greeting. "Yo, *what*?"

From Keith's scowl I judged that Major Drummond, the hostage negotiator, was telling Keith that there were going to be delays, that coming up with a billion dollars by five-fifteen in the morning might be a minor problem, that sort of thing.

While he was going back and forth with the hostage negotiator, I heard something, a soft scraping noise on the ceiling above us. At first I thought maybe it was a rat. But the more I listened to the deliberate scrape and pause, scrape and pause, the more I was sure it was no rodent. There was a squeak, too, of roof timbers flexing under a lot of weight. No, it was some SWAT guy working his way across the roof.

I was not hot on the idea of a bunch of heavily armed cops guys busting in the door. But the more I watched Keith, the more he scared me. He was obviously pretty deep into his stash of crystal meth by now—and the more of that stuff you used, the less predictable you were, the quicker to anger, the more likely to kill somebody for no good reason. Especially in a pressure cooker situation like this.

After a couple of minutes I realized that Keith had heard the noise, too. He had picked up the phone, tucked it under his left arm, the receiver in his left hand, dragging the cord down the middle of the café. He was still talking on the phone, but he had his gun pointed up at the ceiling toward the source of the noise.

Earlier when I had talked to Major Drummond, he had given me a direct line for reaching him. I ducked under the table where I was sitting and dialed the number.

"Sergeant Williams," a man's voice said.

"This is Sunny Childs," I whispered. "Tell Drummond to get the man off the roof."

"What? I can't hear you."

"Get the man off the roof!" I hissed. "Keith's about to shoot him."

"Who's Keith?"

"The gunman inside. His real name is Keith Trice. Get the SWAT guy off the roof before—"

But Keith was already shooting. The loud smack of the gun filled the room. One shot. Two.

Then footsteps on the roof as the policeman sprang to his feet and ran for it. I just hoped he hadn't been hurt.

I tucked my cell phone back in my pocket.

"Yeeeeeeee-ah!" Keith yelled. "That's right! How 'bout some of *that*, huh, dog? Huh?"

He hurled the phone at the floor, where it splintered into three or four pieces of jagged plastic and cheap circuitry.

I don't know what it is about gunshots, but it was like the sound had frozen, lodged in my chest, clenching up the muscles that allowed me to breathe.

"You're not helping yourself if you kill a cop, Keith," I said.

Keith stared at me for a long time, his eyes hot with adrenaline and crank. "How you know my name?" he said finally.

I don't know why exactly, but I didn't want to throw

Shana under the bus on this one. "You told the police negotiator. On the phone. I overheard you."

"I ain't told no cops my name!"

"Well, actually, yeah you did," I said, smiling apologetically. "I mean, where else would I have found out?"

He kept staring at me. Finally a nervous, self-doubting cloud seeped into his eyes. "I told the cops my *name*? Dayum! I can't believe I told the cops my . . ." He broke off in midsentence and then suddenly shook his head, as though to clear his mind.

"A'ight, a'ight." The kid motioned to me. "Come back to the storeroom with me." I followed him back behind the counter. He motioned me to go in while he kept an eye on his hostages. "Look around in here, see if you can find something that'll burn. Gasoline preferably. But it could be anything. Kerosene, propane, anything."

"Why?"

He glared at me. " 'Cause I damn said to."

I stifled my impulse to smart-mouth him and started looking around the room in a desultory fashion. There were shelves on three walls of the room, and boxes stacked up higgledy-piggledy, so it took me a while.

"Look," I said after I'd hunted through a few industrial sized boxes filled with potato chips or bags of flour or paper napkins or coffee filters, "if there was gasoline in here, don't you think it would be obvious?"

Keith peered around the room and then said, "What about that? Looks like a bunch of kerosene to me."

I looked where he was pointing. On the bottom shelf of the room, tucked behind a jumble of boxes and bags in the far back corner, was a two-gallon tin jug, the kind they sell kerosene in. *Why would they have kerosene here, though?* I wondered.

I pulled aside several boxes, and there on the bottom shelf was not just one, but an entire row of gleaming tin jugs with screw tops. But they weren't kerosene. The labels on the side said ETHER. Underneath that in large red print were the words DANGER! FLAMMABLE!

"Ether!" Keith Trice said, grinning. "That'll work perfect."

"Now what?"

"Go out and get Loretta Lynn to open up all the milk jugs in this joint, pour out the milk, fill them with ether."

I didn't like where this was going. But what could I do? I went out and asked Loretta Lynn to show me where they kept the milk.

She pointed to a refrigerator behind the counter. I opened it, took out four jugs of whole milk, and emptied them out.

"Now what?" I said.

"Fill them with ether."

I did as I was told, carrying the tins of ether out to the counter, filling the milk jugs with the clear volatile liquid from the tins.

"Duct tape!" Keith called to me. "Everybody in the world gots duct tape."

I looked at Loretta Lynn. She pointed at the counter. There on the same shelf as the toolbox lay a staple gun, a rectangular piece of cardboard covered with thumbtacks, a piece of green chalk, and a roll of duct tape.

While I was working, Keith stood up on one of the empty tables, unscrewed the lightbulb, then smashed it with the barrel of his pistol.

"Where's the light switch, Loretta?" Keith said.

"They's a fuse box over here," Loretta Lynn said, pointing to a gray metal panel on the wall toward the back of the counter, next to the door to the storeroom.

"Turn off the switch for this light."

"It'll shut off all the lights over all the tables."

"Just do it."

Loretta opened the fuse box, flipped a breaker, and the room went dim. There were still lights over the grill and the counter, but all lights hanging over the booths had gone dark.

Keith walked over to me with the lightbulb he'd just smashed and handed it to me. I saw that—although the glass was smashed—the filament was still intact. "A'ight, Sunny," Keith said. "What I want you to do now is attach this here lightbulb inside the neck of this milk jug. Use however much tape you need. But whatever you do, don't break this part."

He watched me intently as I put the filament into the neck of the bottle, then ran loop after loop of tape around the jug.

"Okay," I said.

"Now screw the whole thing back into the socket over there and then tape it onto the chandelier so it won't fall off. I could see what he was doing now. It was ingenious, I had to admit—especially for a nitwit like Keith Trice.

After I'd put the first apparatus together, he had me repeat the same process with another smashed lightbulb, another milk jug full of ether, and another light socket.

"Cool," Keith said. "Now go hang them other two jugs over the doors, hang 'em up so that if somebody busts the door down, that ether'll spill all over the place."

I nodded, did as I was told.

Maybe I'd underestimated this kid. Suddenly he wasn't seeming quite as dumb as he had earlier. I guess the old saw about necessity being the mother of invention applies even to nitwits.

Keith walked over to the phone as soon as I was done, dialed zero, and waited a couple of moments. "Hi there, Major," Keith said. "Nah. Nah. I keep telling you, I ain't kill that lady. Hey! Shut up. Reason I'm calling you, something you need to know. I now gots this place wired up so if you blow the doors off or be busting in here or anything, the place go up like a *bomb* gotdamn it." He grinned and looked over at the clock on the wall by the chalkboard with the specials written on it. "Five-fifteen, Major. That gives you a hour and forty-five minutes to get me my billion dollars. Bye-bye."

He slammed down the phone, grinned, took a few swats at the air. "*Master* criminal! Yeeee-ah!"

CHAPTER 12

"THERE'S SOMETHING I haven't told you about Jim," Esther said, continuing with her story. "Jim was born in Cabbagetown. Smart young man. Vigorous, highly motivated."

Keith Trice was pacing up and down next to Esther's booth, listening as she continued with her story. His braids kept falling in his eyes and he would brush them back and they would fall, over and over, the same back-handed gesture.

"Jim was valedictorian at his high school, king of the prom, cocaptain of the football team, dated the prettiest girl in the school, went to Georgia Tech on full scholarship, got a civil engineering degree, came out and became a construction supervisor for one of these big outfits that builds roads.

"But all the time, he was dissatisfied. Not only dissatisfied, but . . . well, on some level he felt like a bit of a fraud. On some level he felt like perhaps he'd risen above his station. His father was a terrible drunk, you see. Belittled Jim when he was a boy, told him he'd never amount to anything, that people from Cabbagetown were worthless, the usual sad story. It had always been a motivator for Jim. Until he fell on the job and hurt his back.

For a few months he had sat around, eager to get back to work . . . and then as the case dragged on and it became clear that he was going to have to malinger a bit if he was to expect a decent settlement, a peculiar sort of lassitude had settled over him.

"He moved to a small trailer park in an outlying suburb of Atlanta. The town of Smyrna, let's say. He drank more than was prudent. He stopped seeing his successful friends, his fraternity brothers and so on. He began doing, essentially, nothing. And what frightened him was that it all seemed so natural. And so this fear had begun rising in him, a fear that perhaps it was in the blood, his father's shiftlessness, that he was now at long last settling back to his natural level in the world.

"So when this strange matter of David Hicks came up, it took him a little by surprise. It exerted a pull on him, you see, as though David Hicks, whoever he was, was trying to reach out of the ether and pull him from this state of torpor into which he had sunk.

"Well, at any rate, the next morning Jim drove down to the county library and looked through the newspapers from 1954, where he found a series of articles about the disappearance of David Hicks. Twelve years old, came home on the school bus, got off half a block down from his house, never seen again.

"There was some brief suspicion of his stepfather, but nothing came of that. A strange Packard had been seen driving slowly through the neighborhood. Nothing came of that. The articles about the disappearance began on September 14th and by October there was no more mention of the matter. David Hicks, so far as the world was concerned, had ceased to exist.

"While Hicks is sitting in the library, he is approached by an attractive young woman who asks for help using the microfilm machine. Next thing you know, they've struck up a conversation and phone numbers are traded. Later that day he calls her up and asks for a date. She is rather unpleasant and declines.

"That evening Jim turns on the television and finds that David Hicks, the young man he had spoken to that afternoon, has died. Accidentally shot through the head while hunting. The witness, according to the newsman: the dead man's uncle. Whose name, as it happens, is also David Hicks."

Keith Trice interrupted. "Hey, yo! I thought David Hicks be dead."

Esther raised her eyebrows. "Well, it is puzzling, isn't it?"

Keith wasn't overstating things to the hostage negotiator. Ether is an extremely volatile and extremely flammable liquid. I happen to know this from personal experience. In college a friend of mine had a work-study job in the bio lab—a job which included drying test tubes with ether after they'd been run through the steam cleaner. She thought she was too cool to concern herself with the laws of chemistry, so she lit a cigarette while sloshing ether around in the test tube. She was lucky: the resulting explosion only gave her second-degree burns on half her body. The doctor told her later that a kid who'd done the same trick at Penn State the previous year had died.

The way Keith had set things up, all he had to do was flip a switch and the two milk jugs hanging from the light fixtures would catch fire. The fire would melt the jugs, showering the room with rapidly vaporizing ether, which would immediately explode.

We were now sitting, quite literally, in the middle of a bomb.

Beyond that, though, there was something else bothering me. Ether? Why did a little greasy spoon have twenty gallons of ether stored in the back. They sure weren't using it to clean out test tubes.

"Okay, Keith," I said. "Got a couple things I need to talk to Lorretta Lynn about."

Keith shrugged. "Whatever."

"But before I do, there's something I need to check out in the storeroom."

He followed me back so that he could watch me. I started opening boxes methodically, searching for something. I finally found it right there in front of me. All morning I'd been sitting on the box of toilet paper. I found the answer right there in the box.

"You got the sniffles?" I said.

Keith Trice looked at me blankly. "Huh?"

"Nothing. Tell Loretta Lynn to get back here," I said.

"Quick question," I said.

The waitress smiled obligingly, patted her large pile of black hair.

"The Blind Pig," I said. "Is it open all week?"

"Except Sunday," she said.

"So this place is empty on Sunday. Nobody using the grill, nobody using the stove?"

She squinted at me with a curious expression. "I guess not."

"Nobody comes in at all?"

"Maybe the owner."

"I see." I looked around the room. "So y'all keep a lot of stuff here in this storeroom, huh?"

"That's what it's for. Keeping stuff."

"Coffee filters. Pancake mix. Toilet paper." I picked up a few items off the shelves, then reached into the industrial sized box of toilet paper and took out a roll of toilet paper. "So, hey, have you got a lot of customers with the sniffles? Lot of colds going around this time of year?"

Suddenly she wasn't looking so obliging.

I threw the toilet paper roll on the floor, then reached deeper into the box of toilet paper. Underneath the layer of toilet paper rolls was something else, something that was definitely not toilet paper. I tossed a few rolls of toilet paper on the floor, exposing row after row of blue boxes, their labels printed in Spanish. I pulled one out and read the label. You didn't even need high school Spanish to figure out what it was. "This is a cold medicine, isn't it? Sniffles, postnasal drip, that kind of thing?"

She shrugged, a cool expression on her face.

"Producto Mexico. That means 'made in Mexico.' "

"So?"

"Why would a place like this have about ten gallons of Mexican cold medicine in the back room? Can you tell me that?" I peered at the side of the box. "Active ingredient here, let's see, something called pseudophedrine hydrochloride. You know what that is?"

Another diffident shrug.

"It's an antihistamine. But it's also a precursor chemical to ephedrine. Which in turn is a prearsor to . . . well, let's put it this way: if you dissolve a pseudophedrine-based medicine in ether, heat it, perform a few other bits of simple home chemistry to it, guess what you end up with?"

Loretta Lynn looked off into the distance.

"Methamphetamines, Loretta Lynn," I said. "Crystal meth. Crank. Speed."

"Well, I don't work here Sundays," she said in a brittle voice. "I wouldn't know nothing about that."

"Who *does* work Sundays?"

"I told you I don't know nothing about that."

"Loretta Lynn, nobody's gonna give this moron a billion dollars. Nobody's gonna land a chopper out on that street. If I don't figure out who killed Phyllis, we're all dead. You understand that, don't you?"

She pressed her brightly colored lips together. Her lipstick had wicked up into the myriad of wrinkles around her mouth so that her mouth had taken on a blurry quality, like a slightly out-of-focus photograph. "That boy killed her."

"I don't think so, Loretta Lynn."

"Then who?"

"That's what I'm trying to find out."

"So you got a theory?"

"Okay, here's one. Suppose whoever owns this place was manufacturing crystal meth here for Shana and Derl. Suppose Phyllis was trying to put the Blind Pig out of business. Maybe Derl wanted to get rid of her. Maybe she was putting the squeeze on Bobby."

"Nope," Loretta Lynn said.

"You're sure of this?"

"I told you, far as I know, only one person come in here on Sundays. That's the owner."

"I don't follow you."

Loretta Lynn laughed bitterly. "Who you think owns the Blind Pig, girl? Phyllis."

"*Phyllis* was manufacturing drugs for Shana and Derl?"

"You said it, not me. I don't know nothing from nothing about no drugs."

I stared at her for a long time. Then I stuck my head out the doorway. "Hey! Superstar. You and me need to have another talk."

CHAPTER 13

KEITH AND I sat next to each other at the end of the counter, away from the rest of the hostages.

"Whassup, baby?" Keith said.

"Okay, first, don't call me baby. I'm thirty-four years old, you're—what? Twelve?"

"I'm nineteen!" he said stiffly.

"There you go. Anyway, that's not my main point. My main point is this. I want you to tell me, no bullshit this time, how you came to hold this place up and what you expected to find here."

He straightened up in his seat. "Girl, don't play me like that!"

"Spare me the attitude," I snapped. "Seriously. What's going on here?"

He sighed looked at the floor for a moment. "A'ight. A'ight. This dude I met on the street set this thing up. Like I said. Only difference from what I originally told you, he said this place had some kind of drug thing going on in it. Said this place had some serious ka-ching in it. Like maybe ten, twenty grand. Otherwise it was just like I said before: he told me they kept all this money in the egg box up there."

"And this guy, you said his name was John Smith. Can you do a little better than that?"

"A'ight. A'ight. His name was Rudolph. Like the reindeer."

"What did he look like?"

Keith shrugged. "White dude. Middle-aged. Had a goatee and long hair, going a little gray."

"You don't know his last name?"

Keith shook his head, then squinted at me. "How come you need to know all this stuff?"

I lowered my voice so nobody else in the room could hear me. "If I'm right, you were sent in here to provide a distraction while somebody else knocked off Phyllis. You ever heard of a 'fall guy'? That's you."

He kept looking at me with those same blank gray eyes.

"How long would you estimate elapsed between the time you fired off those shots and the time the cops rolled up here? Thirty seconds? A minute? Even if somebody had called 911 the second you walked in, the police would never have gotten here *that* fast.

"You saying Rudolph set me up." The poor moron was finally getting it.

"I'm saying most likely somebody paid Rudolph to set you up. So if we could find out who paid Rudolph, we'd know who set this thing up."

"Only Rudolph ain't here."

I nodded. "So we have to crack this nut some other way."

"How you gonna do that?"

"Somebody here had a reason to want Phyllis dead. We just need to draw that person out."

"And how we gonna do that?"

"I'm thinking about that," I said. "Meanwhile, can I use the bathroom?"

Keith eyed me suspiciously. "Well, don't take too long."

He followed me back to the bathroom, watched me as I went in.

"You mind?" I said.

Keith gave me a stare, then pimp-strutted back up the aisle. As soon as I'd closed the door, I called Barrington on my cell phone.

"Got something quick for you to check out. Can you hotfoot it over to that homeless shelter, the Atlanta Mission over on Ponce de Leon, see if you can find a guy named Rudolph. Sounds like somebody hired him to set up this heist. I want to know who it was."

CHAPTER 14

AS I POKED my head back out of the tiny room, Keith Trice was up in the front of the café, where he was doing bogus karate moves, spinning around, making squinty-eyed Bruce Lee faces, bludgeoning awkwardly at the air. I presumed he had just taken another hit of amphetamines and was working off the burst of energy.

Patrick, the yuppie artist, was watching him with a disdainful expression on his face. After a moment, he snickered loudly.

Keith Trice broke off his theatrics, turned toward Patrick, and gave him a hard stare. "Something funny, dude?"

Patrick looked at him straight-faced and said, "Oh, I was just wondering where you learned all that stuff."

"This?" Keith spun around, doing a pathetic hook kick, then punched feebly at the air. The move was accompanied by a loud scream and a Bruce Lee grimace.

Patrick nodded. "That, yeah."

"I took a little Tae Kwon Do, you know what I'm saying." Keith looked smug.

"That right?" There was something going on behind Patrick's eyes, but I couldn't tell what it was. His wife was looking at him with an expression that might have been loathing or might have been fear. "What rank did you earn?"

"Me?" Keith raised his eyebrows. "I'm . . . yeah, I'm a black belt. Ninth degree."

This, of course, was ludicrous. Even in Tae Kwon Do, where rank inflation is rampant, no nineteen-year-old was going to be a ninth degree black belt.

"I guess you were part of the Pan-American Tae Kwon Do Federation?" Patrick said pleasantly.

"Oh, yeah. I was way up there. Right up in the top ten guys."

Patrick looked at him for a moment. "You poser," he said finally. "There's no such thing as the Pan-American Tae Kwon Do Federation."

Keith Trice looked back at Patrick for a minute, his face flushed. His fingers of one hand were jitterbugging on the counter and there was a tiny tremor in a muscle under his eye. "You know something, dog?" Keith said. "I'm fixing to get tired of you."

Patrick shrugged slightly. "And?"

Patrick's wife shook her head slightly, staring at him, aghast. "What's wrong with you, Patrick?" she said softly.

"What's *wrong* with me?" Patrick smiled tightly and looked around the café. "What wrong with *me*? What's wrong with me, is that I'm tired of listening to this idiot up there. Just because you have a gun, you think you can tell everybody in here what to do. Well, I for one have had it up to here!"

Keith Trice's eyes were narrow now. He walked slowly back toward Patrick. Patrick stood up to meet him. From where I stood I noticed something about Patrick that I hadn't seen before. The first knuckles of his index and middle fingers on both hands were ridged with a heavy callus. There was only one way you got calluses like that: it came from pounding a martial arts training device called a *makiwara*. Obviously Patrick had some martial arts experience.

"You're a big man as long as you got that gun," Patrick

said. "How about you show off some of your karate talents? Huh? You're the big karate pimp hustler superstar bad-ass; me, I'm just some yuppy wuss writer. Come on, home boy. Show us your stuff." I was right: Patrick was hoping to convince Keith to set down the gun so he could unload some karate on the guy. It was a bad idea to begin with. And by revealing his knowledge about martial arts, he'd already tipped his hand.

"Hey," I said, "come on guys. Let's chill for a minute."

But the testosterone was running way too high by then: they ignored me.

"Come on, Superstar. Show me how it's done."

But Keith Trice had seen through Patrick's ruse. He may have been dumb, but he wasn't *that* dumb. Derl had already tried it once. I couldn't see why Patrick thought he'd fall for it a second time. He pointed his gun at Patrick's wife, Connie.

"Don't you wish, you bastard," she said. And it was obvious she wasn't talking to the gunman. She had a furious smile frozen on her face and she shook her head slightly. "You'd just love it if he shot me."

But Patrick refused to back down. "Come on, man!" he yelled, his voice cracking. "You want to show how tough you are? Huh? Huh? Put the gun down and show me."

Keith was obviously torn. He wasn't going to fight Patrick, who was bigger and older and, no doubt, better trained. But he didn't want to look weak either. His finger tightened on the trigger.

Then something unexpected happened.

"Hey!" It was Shana coming out from behind me. "Hey, y'all, that's about enough." She strode up the aisle, grabbed Patrick by his collar, and jerked his head backward. Because she had caught him unawares, she was able to shove the much larger and stronger Patrick into the booth before he could react. "No need of everybody getting all het up over nothing." She had a genial smile on her face, but she sat down next to him hard, jamming him against the wall so he couldn't get out of the seat.

The whole thing took me by surprise because I hadn't seen her as the altruistic type. Superstar was still pointing the gun at Connie, who had slid down in her seat a little.

"Why don't you apologize, Patrick?" Shana said pleasantly but insistently. "We're all a little wired right now, tempers getting high, no need of nobody getting shot over it."

Patrick looked down shamefacedly.

"Patrick? Come on."

Patrick ran one hand slowly across the green formica tabletop. He didn't meet anyone's eyes. "Sorry, man. Guess I got a little worked up."

Keith leaned his head back a little, lowered his eyelids, and waggled his gun at Connie's glossy black hair. "You know *that's* right. 'Cause next time, I'ma cap this ho."

I seized the moment to say, "Okay, Keith, it's time for me to interview the next person."

Keith glared at me. "Who you want to talk to?"

"How about her?" I nodded in Connie's direction. "And how about not pointing the gun at her now?"

Superstar gave me a hard look, then gestured at Connie with the gun. "You heard the lady. Let's go, bay-bee."

"Somebody's going to get shot pretty soon," I said once we were back in the storage room.

Connie scowled but didn't reply, instead just looking off into the distance.

"Did you see the shooting?" I said. "This kid, Superstar, he says he didn't shoot the victim. Did you see what happened?"

Connie didn't seem to be paying me any attention. Her mind was elsewhere.

"Cabbagetown," she said finally, trailing the word out in a long slow parade of angry little syllables.

I waited.

"This whole thing was Patrick's brilliant idea," she said finally. She swallowed and cleared her throat, but her mouth seemed to have gone dry. "I wanted to move out to Alpharetta or Sandy Springs—someplace safe and sensible. We could have afforded a perfectly nice place. Okay, I would have had a commute, but I could live with that." She sneered. "But no, Patrick thinks the suburbs are too *sterile*. Too *white-bread*. Too bland, too bourgeois, too . . . whatever."

She paused.

"I really don't know what happened. When we got married, he was writing ad copy. Good copywriter, too, well respected. But suddenly, about a year after we get married, he tells me he wants something different. Says he wants to be a 'real' writer." She squinted as though trying to understand something. "I mean he used to talk about being a *real* writer in this vague sort of way. Talking about this novel he wanted to write someday. But everybody talks . . . don't they?" She looked at me curiously. "Everybody says, 'Oh, yeah, I'm going to quit my job and move to Tahiti.' But they're not serious. Right?"

I didn't answer.

"Well, come to find out, Patrick *is* serious. He walks in one day, about a year after we've been married, with this shit-eating grin, and tells me he's quit his job. Boom! Surprise, honey! Come to find out he doesn't think having a normal job is 'real' work. Come to find out the nine-to-five world is all some kind of big scam perpetrated by Madison Avenue, blah blah blah. No, I find out that to him 'real' work means quitting your job, throwing away your steady paycheck, and just, you know, doing some kind of Emersonian be-you-own-person thing.

"But who am I to cramp his style? He says to me 'I'm a writer, Connie.' Okay, fine. He's a writer. So we come up with this plan. Or, *he* comes up with a plan anyway. The idea was that we'd buy a place on the cheap here in Cabbagetown, then he'd work on his novel in the mornings, and fix up the house in the afternoons."

"At first it seemed kind of exciting. The first week, he tore out all the walls, and put in all this plastic sheeting. Great. Progress. It's a little tacky, but hey, pretty soon it'll all be better, right?" She grimaced sarcastically. "Well, guess what? It's eighteen months later and I'm still living inside a wreck full of sawdust and naked two-by-fours and plastic sheeting.

"And where's the novel? Gosh, I have no idea. I come home, and I say, 'Patrick, how's the book coming?' And he looks at me like I pooped in his Easter basket. Why? Because apparently it cramps his style. I'm 'measuring' him. I'm 'judging' him. I'm . . . I forget all the other words to describe what a shrew I am, but basically I'm imposing all my narrow bourgeois notions about getting off your ass and accomplishing things on what is apparently a very free-form, amorphous, endless, measureless process that can't be rushed. Okay fine, Patrick. Take your time with the book. But could you at least, after eighteen months, manage to put a flush toilet in our bathroom?"

Her eyes started to tear up a little. "What does this guy do all day? I go to work, I practice law, I bust my butt, I bring home a regular paycheck. That's what I'm doing eight, ten, twelve hours a day. But what does *he* do all day? It's a mystery. It's a great big whopping mystery. And he won't tell me. But whatever it is, it's not writing the great American novel and it's not hanging drywall."

I decided to try a new tack, since I hadn't gotten very far with my first question. "Did Patrick know Phyllis McClint?"

Connie looked up at me sharply as though noticing me for the first time. "Sure. She sold us the house."

"And have you dealt with her since?"

"She runs POCA, the neighborhood association. We're members, so, sure, we've dealt with her."

"Did you like her?"

"For selling me the house, alone, I could kill her." Connie ran her hand through her glossy black hair. "Seriously, though, I'm not her biggest fan, no."

"Why not?"

"She was loud, crude, and abrasive." She shrugged. "But . . ."

"But what?"

"Look, some people are useful but unpleasant, you know what I mean? She was like a necessary evil."

"How so?"

"Have you looked around this place? A bunch of red-necks living in the middle of a black ghetto next to a mill that shut down three decades back? The writing was on the wall a long, long, long time ago. This place has out-lived its usefulness. Phyllis figured that out. And she's figured out that to make a reasonably graceful transition from what the neighborhood used to be, to what it will be—well, you have to do certain things."

"Such as?"

"Getting rid of crime. Sprucing things up. Hitting up city hall and HUD for matching funds and low-interest loans."

"And convincing the original residents to move out?"

A tiny glimmer of a smile. "That too."

"So, did you see anybody shoot Phyllis? Besides this kid who held up the place, I mean?"

"I was facing the wrong way. I just heard all this yelling then shots, then the lights went out, and then there was something wet on the side of my face. I didn't figure out until later that it was blood." She touched her face un-consciously. She'd obviously swabbed her face off with her napkin or her sleeve or something, but there were still a few reddish brown smears above her left eyebrow.

"Okay, you heard yelling, then shots?"

"I don't want to think about it."

"Please."

She sighed heavily. "He was yelling. 'Give me the money,' that sort of thing. Then there were, let's see . . ." She squeezed her eyes shut. "A bunch of shots. Then a flash. Lightning, I guess. Then the lights went out. Then there was this huge crash of thunder. Then a few seconds later the lights came on and there was one more bang. Then I felt the wetness on my . . ." She shuddered, break-ing off in midsentence.

"That last bang. Where did it come from?"

"I don't know. My ears are still ringing."

"Did it seem to come from a different part of the café?"

Connie bit her lip. "Maybe." She shook her head. "No. I mean . . . I don't know. I had my head covered. It seemed really loud, really close. But maybe he just moved."

"So you weren't looking around you?"

"No."

"How many shots did you hear?"

Connie closed her eyes. Her lips moved and she counted the shots off on her fingers. "Three."

"You sure?"

"Three shots, then the lights went out, then the fourth shot."

I had about run out of questions when I heard someone yelling from out in the restaurant. "Hey! Hey! Look!"

I poked my head outside the storeroom. Keith Trice was pointing his fingers at something on the floor.

"What?" I said.

"Look, Sunny. Come look."

I ran down the length of the restaurant. There, lying on the floor, pushed up against the wall at Patrick's feet was a gun.

"Pick it up, dude," Keith Trice shouted to Patrick. "Real slow. Just hook your pinky finger into the trigger guard and haul it out. Get cute, I'ma kill you."

Patrick did as he was told, leaning over to collect the pistol, then straightening up with the gun hanging on his finger. It was a compact automatic, black, with some kind of custom grip on it. Keith reached forward and snatched it out of Patrick's hand.

"Lookie there, homes," Keith Trice said. He indicated something else, pointing at the table with his gun.

"What?" I said.

He just kept pointing.

Then I saw it. Lying on the table behind the saltshaker, behind the plastic caddy full of blister-packs of jelly and whipped margarine, lay a small brass cartridge.

"I want you to take a Polaroid of that, man. See? See, that proves what I been saying all this time."

Just then my cell phone began to ring. I looked around, trying to act like I didn't know where it was coming from.

Keith Trice stared at me, stepped backward a half step as though I'd slapped him. "You had a *phone*? I *trusted* you! All this time you had a *phone*?"

CHAPTER 15

THE CELL PHONE kept ringing.

Keith stepped forward, shoved me hard into the table, thrust one leg between my thighs so I couldn't maneuver, then reached into my pocket and grabbed the phone.

"You been talking to the cops, haven't you? Huh? Huh, bi-yetch?"

"Look, no, I—"

The phone rang and rang, and Keith ground my hips savagely against Patrick's table.

"I swear . . ." I said.

"I'ma answer it," Keith said. "If it's the cops, you in deep deep deep doo-doo." He flipped open the phone. "Yeah?"

He glared at me, then frowned. Then nodded.

"No!" he said. Then, after a brief pause, "Look, lady . . . Hey, look, no. Uh-huh. Uh-huh." More nodding, then finally his face took on a defensive quality. "Yes ma'am. Well, yeah, but . . . Yeah but . . . Well, I didn't come in to . . . I know that. It just got out of control, you know what I'm saying? Yes ma'am. Yes ma'am." He sighed loudly, then handed me the phone.

"Who is it?" I said.

"It's your mama."

I grabbed the phone. Mom. It figured. She had a way of involving herself in things at the most inopportune times. "Mother! Uh, now's not good. I've kind of been taken hostage."

"I know that, dear," my mother said cheerily. "It's on the TV. They said there was a girl private eye in there, and I figured it had to be you."

"It's two o'clock in the morning. Why aren't you asleep?"

"Just got back from a charity thing. Anyway, that's not why I called. I figured that if you were in a jam, you'd need help, so I called Gunnar." Gunnar Brushwood is my boss, head of Peachtree Investigations.

"Well, that's nice, Mom, but there's really not much he can do to help."

"Nonsense, darling. He's very experienced in these sorts of matters. I've got him on a conference call. Go ahead, Gunnar."

Like my mother, Gunnar Brushwood has the sort of room-filling personality that you don't necessarily feel like dealing with when someone is holding a gun to your head.

"Hey, doll," Gunnar said. "You holding up all right?"

"I was until you called."

"Sorry about that. I didn't know your mama was going to call you directly. I'd have advised against it. But now that it's done, is there anything I can do to help?"

"I'm in a tiny building surrounded by trigger-happy cops with machine guns. All the doors are nailed shut and a guy is pointing a gun at my head. Do you see any way that you can help?"

Gunnar hesitated. "I'm just asking," he said gently in his deep rumbling voice. Actually, I have to admit, it was kind of nice to be talking to somebody outside the café, somebody who seemed older and, well, more responsible.

Keith Trice nudged me. "Hang up!" he said. "That's long enough. I don't want your mama passing on no information to the cops."

"Hold on," I said. "I just thought of something." I put my hand over the receiver and said, "My mom's not the only person on the line. My boss is on the line, too. He's a gun nut. If you really didn't shoot Phyllis McClint, he may be able to help us figure out what happened here."

Keith Trice's eyes narrowed. "Huh?"

"Ballistics? Tool marks? Forensics? Does any of this stuff ring a bell? This could totally turn the corner for you."

Keith put his hand down the front of his pants, scratched idly as he thought about it. "Okay," he said finally. "But don't try being smart."

I explained the situation to Gunnar, that there were two guns in the café, that Keith claimed he had not shot Phyllis McClint, that we had just found an empty cartridge case on a table.

There was a long pause, then Gunnar said, "All right, darling, I'll walk you through this. Let's see if we can figure anything out. First thing you need to do is tell me about the two guns involved. Make, model, caliber, appearance . . ."

"The guns," I said to Keith. "I need to know what we're dealing with."

Keith scowled. "I ain't giving you my gun if that's what you mean."

Apparently Gunnar overheard him because he said, "Tell this boy to take the magazine of the pistol you just found, set it down, work the slide and clear the magazine so the weapon is empty, then set the gun down a few feet away from the magazine. That way he can let you examine each part separately without fear of you trying to shoot him. When you're done, he reloads that weapon, covers you with it while you examine his pistol."

I explained Gunnar's suggestion and Keith okayed the idea. He pulled out the magazine, racked the slide, set the two items down on the counter about eight feet apart.

"First tell me about the weapon," Gunnar said.

I picked it up, studied it carefully. I know a reasonable

amount about guns, but Gunnar knows a lot more. I figured I'd tell him the facts and let him draw conclusions. "Okay," I said. "This is the pistol we found on the floor. It's an automatic pistol with a blued steel frame. Plastic grips with the letters P239 molded into the handle. On the receiver it says SIG."

"Okay," Gunnar returned. "So that means it's a SIG P239. That's a compact pistol made by an Austrian company, designed for easy carry and concealment. Very nice weapon. Reasonably common, but a little pricey. What caliber?"

Stamped into the slide were the letters 9MM. "It's a nine," I said.

"Okay, smell it."

I sniffed the gun. It smelled of gun oil and burned powder. "Strong odor of gunpowder."

"That means it's been fired relatively recently."

"I'll be damn. How recently?"

"A few hours? A few days? Hard to say."

"Okay. What next?"

"When this kid worked the action, was there a bullet in the chamber?"

"Yes."

"Okay. That's meaningful. When you fire an auto, it reloads the chamber, right? So if there hadn't been a round in the chamber, it would have meant that if somebody had fired it in the restaurant, they would have had to pull the magazine out, work the action, push the magazine back in, then pick up the live cartridge—which would have fallen on the ground."

"In other words, if the chamber had been empty, it would have pretty much ruled this out as a possible murder weapon."

"Right. But since the round *is* in the chamber, it could still be the one."

"Okay. Let's go to the magazine."

I explained what I'd learned to Keith, then set down the pistol and picked up the magazine. It was a more-or-less rectangular box made of sheet steel, about three-quarters of an inch thick, an inch wide, and just over three inches long. Visible through a slot in the side was a stack of bullets. The nose of one round protruded through the top. "Got it," I said.

"First thing, push down on the top round with your thumb. Hard. If there's play, that means that it's not completely full."

I pushed and the stack of bullets moved down. "There's about half an inch of play."

"Okay, take out all the bullets and count them. The magazine should hold eight rounds."

I thumbed out the bullets lined them up on the counter. "Seven."

"Okay. So, that means that the magazine has one round missing. If it was completely full, that would rule this out as having just been fired because as the gun cycled, it would kick a round up into the chamber."

"So you're saying it's possible that this gun was just fired."

"Right."

"Next?"

"Take a look at one of the rounds, tell me about it."

I picked up one of bullets, studied it carefully. The cartridge was bright untarnished brass. The slug was odd looking, not lead but some other material. On the butt of the round were imprinted M-S and 9MM LUGER. I described it to Gunnar.

"Okay," Gunnar said. "That means it's a nine-millimeter round made by a company called Mag-Safe. This is a kind of unusual round. The slug isn't actually a bullet in the normal sense. It's made of a jacketed core of tiny lead shot suspended in epoxy. Lightweight, very high velocity. When the round hits you, it breaks apart and all these little lead balls go smashing around inside you. Tears a great big old hole."

"Okay."

Gunnar's deep voice dropped to a whisper. "Is our boy listening in?"

"No."

"Is the safety on or off?"

"Looks like it's off. It's ready to fire."

"If you can do it unobtrusively, put it on safety again. Just in case."

I did what he suggested, then set the gun down.

"Okay," Gunnar continued, "tell me about the empty cartridge you found on the table."

I went over and picked it up. "Same deal. Mag-Safe nine-millimeter," I said.

"Tell the kid you're ready for the next weapon," Gunnar said.

I handed the weapon back to Keith, who reloaded the weapon we'd found, then unloaded his own pistol and placed the magazine and the weapon separately on the counter.

I picked up the pistol first. "Keith's weapon is an automatic, too. The other one was blued, but this one has a bright metal finish. Nickel or something. Huh. It's a SIG also."

"What model?"

"It says P220 on the handle."

"Okay, that's a much larger model than the P239."

"Yeah," I said. "Longer barrel, heavier."

"Lots more expensive, too. Retails close to a thousand." There was a long pause. "I trust this boy's still not listening in?"

"Right."

"Here's the thing. This is not an uncommon weapon, but it's not the kind of thing your usual 7-11 stickup artist carries. An old-fashioned bank robber, maybe. But guys who stick up retail outlets and stuff like that, they're usually looking to make a quick buck to pay for drugs. If it's in good condition, he could have hocked the gun, picked up a couple hundred bucks. He'd have to hold up three dozen convenience stores just to pay for the weapon."

"Yeah," I said. "I was kind of thinking the same thing. But he says somebody gave it to him."

"Hm," Gunnar said skeptically. "All right, let's take a look at the magazine."

I set the pistol down, picked up the magazine, examined it carefully. "There's a little sticker on the bottom of the magazine that said, RAY'S 24-HOUR GUN & PAWN with an address on Memorial Avenue," I said.

"Excellent. If he bought the gun there, they've got the federal gun buyer's form on file."

"Oh, right," I said. "I didn't even think of that." Everybody who buys a gun fills out a federal form on which they profess not to be a criminal or lunatic. Those forms are then kept on file by the store. "Do me a favor and call Barrington. See if he can't drop by good old Ray. If it's a twenty-four-hour place, he can find out who bought it."

"I'm one step ahead of you, darling."

I thumbed the bullets out of the magazine. "There were two rounds left in the magazine," I said. "They're both identical. It says WIN 9MM LUGER on the bottom. The bullet itself appears to be lead."

"Winchester nine-millimeter. That's a real common round," Gunnar said. "Ask him if he carried a round in the chamber, or if he had to rack the slide before he fired the first round."

I relayed the question to Keith.

He looked up for a moment, thinking, then said, "Yeah, I come in the door, I held up the pistol so they could see it, then I racked that baby and started shooting."

Overhearing the conversation, Gunnar said, "Okay, the P220 also carries eight rounds in the clip. You've got two rounds left. You can confirm this by counting the brass on the floor where he was standing, but it looks like he fired six rounds, total."

"That sounds right. He fired a bunch of shots—maybe three—when he came in, then he fired one round later, when he was trying to get the waitress to give him the money. Then one round when he got annoyed at somebody. Then two more rounds when he heard a SWAT guy on the roof."

"Okay, you can give the pistol back. Now, go stand where he was standing and see how many bullet holes you've got in the ceiling."

First I scanned the floor. Five bright brass cylinders lay on the floor to the left of the register, then a sixth lay under a stool two strides to the right. I picked them all up, lined them up on the counter. They were all Winchester nine-millimeter cartridges. I walked over and looked up at the ancient, sagging, water-stained acoustical ceiling tiles. There were three distinct holes in a three-foot-square area.

"Son of a gun," I said.

"What?" Keith Trice said.

I kept looking at the bullets holes for a moment, then I turned to the kid and said, "I think me and Patrick need to have a little heart-to-heart chat."

CHAPTER 16

I WENT INTO the storage room, then I sat down on a crate and looked at Patrick for a long time.

"What?" he said finally. "You really believe that cretin?"

"You got another explanation?"

Patrick looked at me as though I were a child who was having trouble learning multiplication. "Let's just say for the sake of argument that somebody besides Superfool out there actually shot Phyllis. I'm a nice middle-class guy who's never even had a ticket for jaywalking. Sitting about two feet from me, you've got a this guy Derl—I mean, what kind of name *is* that?—Derl! Derl, I bet he's got a rap sheet as long as your arm. We all know he's a drug dealer. If somebody besides Supermoron did it, it was him. He shoots her, he slides the gun under the table, it ends up under my feet."

"What about the cartridge? It was on *your* table."

"Our booth is directly next to Derl's. Right? The cartridge bounces off the wall, tink, flies onto our table. It's not a billiard ball. It's not going to bounce perfectly straight. After it hit the wall it could have bounced anywhere within, what, eight or ten feet of his booth."

I had to admit it was as plausible as anything else.

"Okay, fair enough," I said. "So let's eliminate you as a suspect then."

"For Chrissake, my wife was sitting right there in front of me. She can tell you I didn't have a gun in my hands."

I just looked at him.

Patrick's brown eyes widened slightly. "Oh, no. Don't tell me."

"She didn't see anything one way or the other. She said she was covering her head with her arms and ducking under the table."

Patrick slumped back in his seat a little, shook his head. "I can't believe this. I can*not* believe this. She was sitting right there!"

I shrugged. "Let's back up," I said. "Just tell me exactly what you saw, what you heard."

"Superdummy comes in the door, points his gun up in the air, fires a couple times, there's a flash of lightning, the lights go out, the lights come back on, Phyllis is running toward him, bang, he shoots her." Patrick extended his arm straight out in front of him and pointed his finger at my head. "That simple."

"You *saw* this."

Patrick tossed his pretty hair. "Of course I saw it. That asshole was standing right there. I don't see how he's got the nerve to deny it."

"I hate to say it, but you're the only person yet who says they actually saw him shoot her. Other than Derl, anyway—and I think he's lying."

"Well, then everybody else in here is blind." He crossed his arms and smiled tightly, as though coming to this conclusion gave him a certain bitter pleasure.

"Anything else you saw? Heard?"

He shook his head.

"Okay. Just to be thorough, you knew Phyllis, right?"

He nodded.

"How?"

"What did my wife tell you?"

I looked at him, puzzled. "What's that got to do with anything?"

"Did she tell you I was having an affair with Phyllis? Is that why you're all suspicious? Because it's not true."

She hadn't said any such thing. But I figured I'd ride this notion see where it led. "Phyllis did get around, Patrick. I gather everybody in Cabbagetown knows this."

"Look, she was an attractive woman. I'll give her that. And, sure, I saw her from time to time. She ran this organization called COPA, and she'd come around the neighborhood occasionally handing out fliers or whatever. I'm a nice guy, I don't mind standing out on the porch jawboning a little. But that was it."

I didn't say a word, just sat there and waited.

Finally Patrick spoke again. "Look, half the people around here are on welfare. They're all sitting around their houses with nothing better to do than spy on their neighbors. Now and then somebody might see Phyllis come to the house. They probably saw her come inside. I might have offered her a glass of wine once or twice . . ."

"Ah. First it's the porch. Then it's coming inside. Then it's having a glass of wine."

Patrick covered his face in his hands for a moment. Then he shook his head. "You have no idea. You have no idea what it's like."

"It?"

"Every day I get up and I go into my office and I sit down and I try to write. Some days I might get five pages out. Some days five sentences. Some days, nothing. A lot of days, actually." He smiled bitterly. "See, Connie doesn't understand what it's like to just jump off the edge with no parachute. She thinks life is supposed to be safe. Easy. No risk. You know, like buying a car with one of these thirty-thousand-mile guarantees and the satellite link so if your engine breaks down, you just push a button and the General Motors Corporation sends help. But writing is not like that. It can't be rushed, it can't be forced, it can't be predicted."

"What's that got to do with Phyllis?"

"Every day she comes home. Connie, I mean. Every evening it's, 'how's the writing going, honey?' " He pinched up his mouth and delivered the last line in a saccharine yet demanding tone. "You know, it's like she wants to verify that I've been productive, that I'm not sitting here spanking the monkey. And if I didn't write a best-selling novel this week, then, hey, why didn't I get the entire house painted and the drywall hung and the bathroom plumbed and the lights wired?"

Patrick closed his eyes, wearily. It seemed suddenly as though the bitterness had drained out of him. "You want to know the truth?" he said softly. "I haven't written a word in six months."

"Writer's block?"

"I guess that's what you'd call it. It's like everything I write totally sucks. I hit this wall and I just can't get past it."

"I don't mean to pry or anything. I'm just curious," I said. "But if you aren't writing and you aren't fixing up the house, then what *are* you doing?"

He shook his head. "I don't know where the time goes, I really don't. You get up nice and early, you run down to some coffee joint, do a little bullshitting over a cup of mochachino, go home, stare at the computer, torture yourself with guilt and boredom and angst or whatever, finally give up on writing and drive over to Home Depot for a piece of wood or a light switch or something, come back, find out it doesn't fit where you want it to, drive back to Home Depot, stop at the grocery on the way back, fix lunch, torture yourself at the computer some more, go to the gym, work out, come home, write a page then nuke it because it sucks, do the laundry, listen to NPR, stare at the computer, fix dinner . . . whammo, the day's all gone. God, Sunny, it's just eating me alive."

He looked up at me, meeting my eye for the first time since we'd come into the storeroom. He had large, liquid brown eyes, the kind my mother calls bedroom eyes. "But

I'll tell you one thing I was not doing. I was not having an affair with Phyllis McClint."

There was something murky in his gaze, though, something I didn't trust. "You sure about that, Patrick?"

He looked away suddenly. When he spoke finally, his voice was all but inaudible. "I love my wife. I really do. We're just . . . something's gone out of true and I don't know what to do about it."

"You didn't answer my question."

He looked at me, eyes wet. "You want me to stand up in front of everybody and say, I had an affair with Phyllis McClint. Well, I'm not going to. Whatever is going on with me, whatever is going on between me and Connie, whatever this dark, stinking, ugly, messed-up thing is that's squatted its hairy ass down on top of my life, the one thing I can tell you for absolute certain is that it's not connected to Phyllis McClint."

"Okay," I said softly.

He wiped his eyes with the ham of one hand, then looked at the floor. "Have you ever tried to do something really hard? I mean *really* hard? Have you ever tried to do something that everybody said would fail, but it's like it's in there pushing up inside of you and there's nothing you can do to stop it, even if it squashes your guts into hamburger? I'm not talking about going to boot camp or medical school or something like that, where somebody's yelling at you all the time, telling you what to do. Writing, *good* writing, man it's like you have to *invent* boot camp from the ground up all by your lonesome." Suddenly he seemed very animated, shaking his finger in the air. "You got to invent the impossible obstacle course, invent the horrible barracks, invent the awful food, invent the hundred-and-two-degree heat, invent marching, invent salutes, invent your own army. All without any models to go by. Then you got to invent the meanest son of a bitch drill instructor in the history of the world. Then you just stand that bastard up on his feet and say, 'Here you go, Sergeant, beat the crap out of me.' And he does it. Beats you down, day after day, telling you you're a loser, a weakling, a fake, a sissy, a nothing, that you'll wash out pretty soon and everybody will just laugh and say they told you so. That's what writing's like. *Real* writing. That's how hard it is."

"Esther Nixon," I said dryly, "is sitting in the middle of a hostage situation and as best I can tell she's using the opportunity to get a head start on her next novel. She seems to bear up fine under the pressure."

Patrick snorted. "Hey, look, nothing against your friend but that's beach reading. Some good-looking woman gets in a predicament, you throw up some obstacles, a little romance, a nasty villain, a little snappy dialogue, presto: beach reading. With a little effort, any jerk can do that. I'm not trying to be snide here, but I have this feeling that there's something inside me that's really valuable. Something that could make a difference to humanity." He flapped his hands at the air helplessly. "See? Listen to that. Just saying it out loud makes me sound like an ass-hole."

"Yeah, it does kind of."

Patrick appraised me for a minute. "See, you don't get it either. You think because I have no schedule, because I can go to Starbucks whenever I want, that I'm just fart-ing around. But it's the psychological pressure of trying to go somewhere nobody else has gone. *That's* what I'm talking about."

"Kind of like *Star Trek*."

Patrick stood up. "Hey, screw it, I don't care what you think. All I'm saying is, Phyllis McClint means zip to me. I got lots bigger stuff to worry about than some real estate hustler with big hair and an overactive libido."

CHAPTER 17

"OCCAM'S RAZOR. HAVE you ever heard of that, young man?"

"Do *what*?" Keith said, flipping a couple of his greasy braids over one ear.

Esther Nixon looked at him steadily. "Occam's razor states, more or less, that the simplest solution to any problem is also the best one. The third law of crime fiction is that Occam's razor is out the window. The solution to any mystery, or the source of danger in any thriller must, of necessity, be the most ingenious, the trickiest, the most bizarre of all possible solutions."

"Huh?"

"Why would a twelve-year-old child disappear?" Esther said. "We all know the answer. In the real world twelve-year-old children disappear because an estranged parent takes them. If, on the other hand, they are taken by a stranger, then that stranger is a sexual deviant.

Keith came over and said, "Is this part of the story?"

"For pity's sake, young man. You asked how to write a novel and I'm telling you." Esther sighed loudly. "Is anyone acquainted with the history of the interstate highway system? Hm? Anyone know its original name?"

"The National Interstate Defense Highway system." I

turned around and saw that it was Reverend Royce Gerrick speaking, the first words he'd said in hours. "It was so we could move armies around in case the Russians attacked."

Esther nodded. "Precisely. Remember, our hero Jim is a construction engineer, a road builder. His mind naturally flows toward areas with which he is familiar. In this case, it occurred to Jim that there was a peculiar coincidence here. The interstate highway system began construction through Atlanta in 1959. David Hicks disappeared in 1959. And the entire block where he lived also disappeared in 1959. Could there be a connection?

"To find out, he went down to the courthouse the next day and began examining plat books for the piece of land where 314 Knight Street was located. He found that in 1959 it had been transferred by eminent domain to the United States government. The previous owner was a Carl Voss. Whom, incidently, Jim knew from his reading, was David Hicks's stepfather.

"Plat books, of course, are arranged geographically. So when you're looking up the owner of record for one property, it's easy enough to look up the records of deeds for adjacent properties. In this case, Jim began flipping from one property to the next. And guess what he found?"

"What?" Keith said.

"The owner of record for the house next door was . . . David Hicks."

"How's that possible?" Keith said. "He was just a kid."

"No, there's a more important question. Upon examining the plat book further, Jim found that all of the properties on the street were owned by companies with names like ABC Properties. But all those companies were listed on the plat books as having the same mailing address. Which was . . . guess what? Three fourteen Knight Street. So the *real* question is: where did Carl Voss get the money to buy up all this property?"

"How do you know—"

"Think about it. David Hicks, a minor, has his name

on the deed to the property closest to 314 Knight Street. Then all the rest of the houses were owned by what were obviously bogus shell companies. There must have been some reason for this. I would hazard this guess. There were certain procedures followed by the federal government in all eminent domain acquisitions, a cross-referencing of names so as to avoid speculators making money by buying and reselling land. If an entire neighborhood were owned by one person, the government would know that some sort of hanky-panky was going on. But suppose you were going to do it anyway, naturally you would buy up the land under false names. Somehow or other, most likely, David Hicks's stepfather found out the highway was coming. So he bought up the house next door under his son's name. Probably a one-time thing. Then—again I'm guessing—he came up with a source of money. At that point, he decided to use shell company names so there was no easy way of connecting him to the buys, and no way for him to get in trouble with the government for illegal speculation."

Keith looked at Esther thoughtfully. "Man, this story's getting boring," he said finally. "You need to have a fight or something. Plus, what happened to the chick in the van?"

"Sunny?" Esther turned to me and gave me an intent look, as though she were trying to convey something to me. But what it was, I wasn't sure. "Where did the money come from? Where did David Hicks's stepfather get the money? I'm going to mull over that question over a cup of coffee. Don't you have more investigating to do?"

"Well, I don't know what else to do," I said. "I've got somebody trying to find out who bought the gun we found on the floor, I've examined the evidence, I've talked to everybody."

"Everybody?" Keith said. "What about him?"

He was pointing to the front of the restaurant. There, looking back at me was the only person I hadn't talked to yet—a small, obese man with a simpleminded smile on his round face. "Oh," I said. "Guess I forgot him."

"Where did the money come from?" Esther said again, still giving me this strange, significant look. "That's what I'm wondering."

CHAPTER 18

THE LITTLE ROLY-POLY man told me his name was Benny Muse. Or maybe it was Mews. I asked him to spell his last name but after the M, he got hung up. He wore thick-framed glasses, one earpiece taped on with surgical tape, that made his eyes appear very large. His oily hair was thin and lay flat on his head, and it was clear he had the mind of a child. He wore overalls that were new, clean, and neatly pressed, with a clean white polyester shirt underneath.

"Where do you live, Benny?"

"Over yonder." He pointed vaguely at the wall. "With my mama, Miss Opal." His voice had a slow, treacly quality. "She's doing right poorly. So I take care of her." He beamed proudly.

"How old are you?"

He poked his tongue out meditatively. "Forty-two? Or either forty . . . uh . . . seven?"

"Do you work around here?"

Benny smiled proudly. "I'm on the disability," he said enthusiastically. "I can't hold down no job, 'cause I get the disability check."

"Okay, Benny, do you know who Phyllis is?"

"I use to be a normal person. When I was a little boy? I had me a coloring book, boy, it was purty. I could color right inside the lines. But they sent me to the facility. Up there at the state. And when I come back I was a disability person. 'Cause of the treatment and all."

"I see. Now I was asking you if you knew Phyllis McClint."

He nodded sadly. "Phyllis is my friend."

"I'm sorry. Did you see what happened to her today?"

"Yeah, she always treat me nice. She give me these." He reached into a small blue backpack, the kind that kids carry to school, and came out with a handful of tiny plastic toy figures, the kind of cheap crap they give away at McDonald's to keep the kids coming back for hamburgers. The toy figures, each of them about an inch and a half tall, were all nasty-looking little animals with buck teeth and crossed eyes and claws and wicked expressions. "This here's Rat-Face. And this one's Bingo. And this one's . . ." He proceeded to tell me the name of each little bucktoothed animal.

"Isn't that cute," I said, then I cleared my throat. "So did you see what happened to Phyllis today?"

"Yes, ma'am," Benny said. "She got shooted."

"Did you see who did it?"

Benny got on his knees, put his toys on top of the box of toilet paper he'd been sitting on, started playing with them intently, making gun noises.

"Benny?"

He pooched out his lower lip, stared intently at his toys. "I ain't seed nothing."

"Benny. If you saw something, you need to tell me."

The retarded man ignored me, still moving his little toys around. "Hey, Rat-Face!" he said in a high voice. "Let's go to the store! Yeah, okay Bingo, let's go buy us a big old Cadillac like Miss Shana drives! Yeah, okay!"

"Benny," I said. "Can you stop playing for a minute?"

"I want to play."

I watched him play intently with his toys, talking in his high-pitched voice. Finally I said, "Can I play too?"

Benny shrugged.

"Here, let's play a game, okay, Benny?" I got down on my knees next to the fat little man. "You ever played restaurant?"

"No ma'am."

"What we're going to do, we're going to pretend all these little guys are people in the café, okay."

"Okay," Benny said dubiously.

I picked up the plastic rat. "Who should this be?"

Benny looked at the rat apprehensively.

"Benny?"

"Superstar," he whispered. "That's the bad man, Superstar."

"Okay, how about this little joker?" I picked up a squirrel with beady little eyes.

"That's Miss Loretta Lynn."

"Hey, you're pretty good at this, Benny."

Benny smiled. "Yeah. Yeah, I'm good at playing restaurant."

We went through all the figures and assigned a name to each of them. The last toy was a skunk which he named Patrick.

"Patrick's a skunk?"

"Yeah. He used to play with me but then he got mean to me."

"Why's that?"

"I seen him and Miss Phyllis doing something nasty in his house. He called me a Pee-Pee Tom."

"A Peeping Tom, you mean?"

"Yeah. A Pee-Pee Tom. Me and him used to play catch sometimes in his yard. But after I seen him and Miss Phyllis doing that nasty thing he wouldn't play with me no more."

"What kind of nasty thing?"

"They had they clothes off. They was hollering and he was hitting her in the butt with his leg."

"He was kicking her?"

"No. Like this here." He stood up and began making awkward but enthusiastic coital motions against me with his hips.

"Okay, okay, okay fine, I get the idea. You can stop now, Benny." When I had finally succeeded in detaching Benny from my leg, I handed the toy rat to him. "So here's Superstar. Let's play the game now. Superstar's coming into the restaurant. I want you to show me what he does when he comes in."

Benny looked at me nervously. "Superstar's fixing to say a dirty word. You gonna wash my mouth out with soap if I say it?"

"No, I'm not going to wash your mouth out. Do you know how to say bad words but not really say them? Like you could say MF instead of a certain bad word or SOB instead of a certain other bad word? Have you ever heard of that?"

Benny smiled a little. "Yeah. Miss Opal does that."

"Miss Opal?"

"My mama."

"Oh, right. I forgot. Anyway, that's fine: try saying it like Miss Opal would say it."

Benny squinted his eyes, put a childishly mean expression on his face, then waggled the little rat around like it was walking across the top of the toilet paper box. "Okay, you MFs, this here's a MF stickup, I'ma kill you MF SOB GD bitches and ho's. Give me the MF money or I'm gonna kill you!" He made a series of explosive noises and jabbed the rat's extended fingers in the air.

Then he picked up the squirrel that was supposed to represent Bobby the grill man and in a high, squeaky voice said, "Here's the money, Superstar."

"Not that money, you MF bitch, give me the money in the MF GD egg box."

"We ain't got no money in no egg box!"

He jabbed the rat at the squirrel, knocking it down. "I want the money in the MF egg box, you bitch."

"We ain't got no money in no egg box!"

"Okay," I interrupted. "That's really good, Benny. You're really good at this game."

Benny smiled proudly. "I know."

"Okay, do you remember how there was lightning?"

"I don't like lighting. It makes me a-scared."

"Me too. But can you show me what happened when the lightning came?"

He made a loud noise and hit the box. All the plastic figures jumped, some of them falling over. "Oh, no!" he squeaked. Then he picked up the white rabbit. "Oh, no, help!"

"The white rabbit, that's Miss Phyllis, right?" I said.

"Yes, ma'am," he said sadly.

"Okay, so are the lights out right now?"

Benny nodded.

"So what happens now?"

He picked up another plastic figure shook it at the white rabbit. *"Pkcheeeeeeeooooo!"* he said.

"Wait a minute," I said. The figure he was holding was a horse with a long yellow mane. Benny had been carrying about fifteen toys in his pocket, some of which were left over. He hadn't assigned a name to this figure. "I think you're getting confused. Who's the horsey?"

"Uh. It's a magic person."

"A magic person."

"Yeah. Like out of the sky or something."

"I don't understand what you mean."

Benny looked frustrated. "In the sky! In the sky!"

"Benny, there aren't any magic people in here. If you saw somebody do it, just tell me. That's how we're playing the game."

"It's only a game?"

"That's right."

" 'Cause I don't want to get nobody in trouble."

I took the horse from him, set it down on the box.

Benny looked down at the toys on the box, picked them up, put them back into the blue backpack. "I ain't like this game," he said. "You don't play no fair."

"Is there somebody else it could have been? Somebody besides the magic horsey from the sky?"

Benny looked at the floor.

"Come on, Benny, this is important."

Benny reached into his book bag, came out with the handful of toys.

"Was it him, Benny?" I pulled out the rat.

Benny shook his head.

"Then who?"

He took the rat back, hunted secretively through the toys, came up with one closed his fist around it so I couldn't see it.

"Is this the one, Benny? In your hand? Is this the one who shot Miss Phyllis?"

He nodded sullenly, his fist still closed around the figure.

"Show me, Benny."

He held his fist closed for a long time.

"You're not making anything up, right? You saw it?"

Benny nodded, his eyes looking at the floor.

"You're sure. You saw the gun and everything?"

He nodded again, then slowly raised his hand, index finger stiff, until his finger was pointing at my neck.

"Show me, Benny. Who shot Phyllis McClint?"

Slowly he rotated his hand until it was palm up, then he unfurled his fingers one by one. Lying in the middle of his soft, fat palm was the small black skunk.

"Patrick," I whispered.

After I was done, I called to Loretta Lynn, "Quick question."

She walked slowly back to the storeroom.

"So what's the scoop with Benny?" I said to the waitress once she'd sat down on the box of toilet paper.

She scratched her head. "He's a retard. If that's what you're getting at."

"What I'm getting at is that he's told me a story, but I don't know whether to believe it or not."

Loretta Lynn closed her eyes, seemed to drift away from me. "You wouldn't think to look at him, but he was the cutest little boy," she said in a dreamy voice. "But weird. And kind of mean, too. They sent him up to the state after he got in some trouble. He didn't come back for a long time. But when he did, you couldn't hardly reconnize him. They'd did something to him up at the state, turned him into a fat little retard. After that he never done a mean thing in his life. So I reckon you could say they done cured him."

"What do you think happened to him?"

"You got me. Electric shock, lobotomy, drugs . . . Whatever they done, though, he come back dumb as a rock."

"So would you trust what he says to be true?"

"Depends. I don't mean he'd intend to deceive you—that ain't in his nature. Plus which, he ain't smart enough to fool you. But I s'pose he could imagine a thing or forget or make something up to please you . . . Anything's possible with Benny."

"What about his memory? You think he can remember things okay?"

"Hard to say. One thing, he got him a head for baseball statistics. You ast him who pitched in the '62 World Series or something, he can tell you. How many balls, how many strikes, how many people he struck out, the whole nine. But then you ast him what time it is, he couldn't tell you to save his life."

"But you don't think he'd intentionally lie or try to get somebody in trouble."

"No, no. He's a sweet little man. Lives with his mama, Miss Opal Terry. She's a shut-in, you don't hardly even see her no more. He buys the groceries, cuts the grass. Takes good care of her. That's a good sign in my book.

Any man takes care of his mama is all right by me. Even if he is a retard."

I figured without more evidence, I might as well disregard him completely. After all, Patrick had been his second choice, after the magic horsey from the sky.

It was while I was sitting there thinking, that something struck me. This whole Scheherazade act that Esther was putting on—why was she doing it? Was she a compulsive storyteller or did she have some other agenda? The way she had been looking at me a few minutes earlier—it just seemed like she was trying to tell me something.

And the answer finally seeped into my thick head. She was trying to circumvent Rule One, Keith Trice's prohibition on our speaking to each other. She was trying to communicate with me. Keith was right, the story she was telling had been interesting at first, but suddenly it got bogged down in all these details about plat books and shell corporations. Could it be she was trying to suggest an avenue of investigation to me?

If so, what was it?

I thought back to what she had been saying. *Where did the money come from?*

Suddenly it hit me. I dialed Barrington again. "Any progress, hon?"

"I took the liberty of running Keith through NCIC," he said. "His nickname says it all: he's a small-time loser, can't get out of his own way. A couple of possession charges, vagrancy, crap like that. Served some county time but that's all. Never committed a violent crime before."

"That seems reasonable."

"Better yet, I tracked down this Rudolph guy. You're right about him getting paid to set this kid Keith up. He said he was approached by a man who gave him two hundred bucks and the gun. He said that the man promised him two hundred more once the robbery went down."

"Did this alleged guy have a name?"

"Nope."

"Description?"

"Kind of vague. White guy. Not young, but not old. Dark hair. Good build."

That could describe about half a million men in the city of Atlanta. Including, for what it was worth, both Derl and Patrick. In a stretch maybe even Reverend Gerrick.

"What about the pawnshop? Did you find out who bought the gun?"

"I'm heading over there right now."

"Great. One last thing. Apparently Phyllis has bought up a bunch of property in Cabbagetown. I can't imagine she's exactly loaded, given that she grew up in this god-forsaken neighborhood and still lives here. Is there any way to figure out where she got all the money from?"

"Depends on your time frame."

"My time frame is, like, right now," I said testily.

Barrington, who is generally a patient guy, said, "Look. Sweetheart. If she bought the property under her own name, we'd have to subpoena her bank records to find out that sort of thing. So you can basically forget it. On the other hand, assuming she bought the property under some sort of corporate shell—and, incidentally, that's the way most developers do it—well, that kind of information is recorded in incorporation records with the Georgia secretary of state." He paused, then in a dry tone of voice added, "It might surprise you to know that the state of Georgia is not open for business at three o'clock in the morning."

"You couldn't, I don't know, hack into a computer or something?"

"When you say you, do you mean *me*? Or do you mean some character actor with funny glasses and wild hair in a Tom Cruise movie?"

I frowned. "Okay, okay. Just go to the pawnshop."

"Yowsah massah."

I should mention, my boyfriend is black. So when he

starts saying things like yowsah massah, I know he's getting particularly pissed.

"Sorry, hon," I said. "It's just—" But I was wasting my breath. The line was dead.

CHAPTER 19

"PRINCIPLE FOUR. THERE must be conflict."

"Like fighting and stuff."

"The woman in the van. Watch this." Esther smiled slyly at Keith. "As Jim pulls a stoplight, the van slides in behind him. Just as—"

Patrick groaned loudly. "Do we *have* to listen to this?"

"Listen to what?" Keith said, annoyed at the interruption.

"Come on, isn't it obvious?" Patrick's tone was hectoring. "The woman in the van is the same girl he met in the library. She's got him under surveillance, right? She's working for the insurance company that he's suing for his disability money. She's trying to see if Jim's malingering. If she can get him on videotape doing something physical, outdoorsy, then his lawsuit goes down the tube. So what's going to happen is that somehow she's going to hook up with Jim and at first there's going to be this big hokey conflict between them and then they're going to fall for each other and then he's going to get in trouble where he needs her help and then she's going to use her superior investigative talents to get him out of the jam. God! It's so *predictable*."

Keith looked blankly at him for a moment, then turned

to Esther with a certain amount of alarm in his eyes. "Is that right?"

Esther smiled thinly at Patrick. "Ah, yes. I overheard you say earlier that you're a writer, too."

Apparently Keith was interested enough in the exchange that he didn't mind the two writers breaking Rule One. "Is that *right*?" he said to Esther. "About the girl in the van?"

Esther laughed dismissively. "Of course he's right. But what makes the story interesting is not what happens, but *how* it happens, *how* the conflict reveals itself."

Patrick snickered disdainfully. "Beach reading," he said.

"If writing beach-reading books were as easy as you seem to think, wouldn't all of us have gotten rich doing it?"

"Some of us think that writing can serve a higher function than titillation, that's all," Patrick said airily.

"Oh, I'm all for higher purposes," Esther said. "Let's hear about your book. I'm sure it would be instructive to us lesser literary lights."

Suddenly Patrick seemed uncomfortable, shifting around in his seat.

"Yeah, dude," Keith said. "Tell us about it."

"Look, good writing is about texture, it's about richness, it's about penetration. Plot is just . . ." He shrugged as though plot didn't even deserve its own disdainful adjective.

"Wait, wait, wait . . ." Esther pressed the back of her hand to her forehead, rolled her eyes to the ceiling. "It's coming to me. Wait . . . Ah! Your novel—it concerns a young man, a sensitive young southerner from a dull, prosperous, and traditional family. Maybe they live in some dry county downstate. Like our hero Jim—he's a star football player, homecoming king, dates the prettiest cheerleader. But, golly gosh, something is missing. He feels out of place in his vapid conservative little town. He has various indeterminate experiences. There's an old man with a foul mouth who drinks corn whiskey and spits blood. There's a dead mule. The boy loses his virginity to a Negro prostitute who works the back room of a county line juke joint. The boy goes to college where he drinks a lot and meets a brilliant scholar—a black man, perhaps, or a Marxist from a northern state? He goes home one weekend and refuses to attend church down at First Baptist. Much familial anguish follows. He graduates. He marries a Jew. He moves to the big city where he works a hateful job and works hard on losing his embarrassingly rural accent. He buys a ramshackle house in a poor neighborhood. He begins to fix up the house— which assumes vaguely mythological and symbolic proportion. The foundations are cracked, the roof is sagging, and there is dry rot in the timbers. He has a brief, stupid affair. His marriage begins to founder." Esther paused, continued to stare fixedly up at the ceiling. "Hmmmmmmm . . . Then, I sense, you begin to run out of ideas. How am I doing?"

Patrick looked at her venomously. The color rising in his cheeks suggested she'd gotten all too close.

"That sounds dull as shit," Keith said.

"Oh, don't be so judgmental, young man. I know, that particular yarn has been written so many times by now that the nap has worn off the velvet a bit. But some people still enjoy that kind of story." Esther pursed her lips, an innocent expression on her face. "Not many. But . . . some."

"Hey, lady," Patrick said. "Fuck you."

Esther smiled pleasantly at Patrick. "You know, my dear, since the very moment I entered this café, I've heard nothing but anger and resentment and pique out of you. It makes me wonder."

"Wonder what?"

"What precisely is it that you're hiding?"

Patrick looked at the older writer with his dark sullen eyes. "Is that some kind of accusation or something?"

Esther opened her eyes wide. "I was thinking more of

something vague—fear of weakness, fear of failure. But now that you mention it . . . there was that cartridge casing on your table."

Patrick looked around the room, a bitter smile on his face. "Oh, I see. I see. Now I'm not just a crummy wannabe writer, I'm a murderer, too."

Esther shrugged.

"Okay, guys," Patrick said. "Y'all think I did it? Huh? What would be the motive? Huh?"

"You did such a nice job figuring out the next twist in my story, perhaps you have a talent for cheesy melodrama," Esther said, her eyes wide with vitriolic fauxinnocence. "Why don't you supply us with a hypothetical motive? Preferably something wonderfully cheap and tawdry."

Patrick said nothing.

"You and Phyllis?" I said, jumping in. "I have a witness."

Patrick's eyes burned into me. "Oh, yeah. A witness. Some moron with an IQ lower than his age, maybe? That's good."

There was a brief pause, then Patrick suddenly looked abashed, realizing what he'd admitted.

"Hey," I said. "You said it, not me. If you know who the witness is, then you know what he saw."

Patrick stared malignantly at me.

Connie was looking at him, and as she did, she seemed to be shrinking up, as though something was just sinking in. He turned toward her. "Oh, come on, Connie. You're going to believe this, this, this . . ." He waved his hand dismissively at Benny.

"Don't," she said softly.

"Connie, please! Give me a break here!"

She turned her face away from him.

Patrick continued to stare at his wife for a long time. The room was entirely silent.

After what seemed a very long time, Patrick stood, spread his arms in the air, rotated them in a slow circle.

"Okay! Congratulations! You win! Everybody wins! I had an affair! Okay! I did the humpy-humpy with Phyllis McClint. Everybody happy now?"

Esther Nixon's eyes were bright.

Patrick's gaze met hers. "Hey, here's a clever little twist, something to pep up my story—which you obviously find to be so trite. Great, let's head straight for the beach-reading market. Maybe Phyllis was going to tell my wife. Here I've been living on the gravy train, my wife supporting me while I'm lazing around the house, spending all day hanging around the coffee shop, and Phyllis was going to blow it for me. Oh, yeah! It makes perfect sense." He got down on his knees, shouting now in a theatrically sarcastic voice. "I confess! I did it! I set it all up in this ridiculously complicated way, hired this insane moron to come in here and fake a robbery, just so I could blow Phyllis away in front of a dozen witnesses!"

The room was quiet for a while.

"There. Is that cheap and tawdry and contrived enough for you?" Patrick said. Then he sat down. In a quiet, spiteful tone, he added, "Thing is, Esther—is that your name? Esther? Thing is, Esther, this is real life. It's not a TV show or some dumb suspense novel where the crotchety old lady solves the crime at the picturesque farm in the Welsh countryside while the full complement of amusing rural types shamble around making themselves out to be suspects. In real life, Occam's razor *does* apply." He pointed his finger at Keith Trice. "A guy comes in here with a gun, fires three shots, the lights go out. There's one more shot. When the lights come on, a woman's dying on the floor. Get real. This genius, this criminal mastermind—*he* shot Phyllis McClint. Any fool on the planet can see it."

He had a point. That was the thing that had been bugging me all this time. If this really was some kind of complicated setup, surely there must have been a better way of doing it. Getting yourself locked in a restaurant with a stupid and unpredictable speed freak like Keith Trice? It just didn't seem smart.

"What about the gun on the floor next to your foot?" I said.

Patrick looked at me and laughed. "So there's a gun on the floor. Big deal. Everybody knows this place is frequented by a bunch of drug-dealing scumbags. Give it a little effort, I bet we could find a whole arsenal in here before the night's over."

There was still one piece of evidence that might, just *might,* sweep away all my doubts. It was a long shot, but still . . . I took out my cell phone. "Mind if I make a call, Keith?"

"Go ahead," the kid said.

I dialed Barrington's car phone. "So was the pawnshop open?"

"Twenty-four hours, baby. A regular Crackheads-R-Us."

"What did you find out?"

"The owner pulled his federal gun-buyer forms. He had a customer for a SIG P239 three weeks ago."

"Who was it?"

Barrington told me. I hung up the phone.

"Okay, Keith," I said. "I'm prepared to make my affidavit to the cops. It looks like you didn't shoot her."

"Yo, who did?"

"My friend went to the pawnshop where the gun was sold, the one we found on the floor. He told me the name of the buyer."

"Give it up, girl!" Keith said.

I turned looked at Patrick.

He blinked, then his eyes widened.

"It won't wash, Patrick," I said. "The gun on the floor is yours."

Patrick kept looking at me. Then something began seeping into his eyes, and he rose out of his chair, dark and furious.

"I'm not going down for this," he said.

"Sit," Keith said softly.

Patrick's voice rose, his eyes searching the room as

though looking for a route of escape. "I'm not going down for this!"

"Don't be stupid, homes." Keith's gun was pointed at the middle of Patrick's chest.

"This is not right! This is not right! I am being *framed*."

"Sit down!" Keith barked, pointing his gun at Patrick. "Sit your ass *down*!" I noticed that all vestiges of his bogus black accent had disappeared under the stress of the moment.

Patrick froze there in the middle of the restaurant. Then he looked around, saw us all staring accusingly at him, and it began to be clear in his mind that he had been cornered, that there was no way out. His eyes desperately sought the one place he thought he could receive some support: his wife.

But Connie was looking back at him with the incredulous expression of someone who has just found out she didn't know the man she loved, didn't know him at all.

Patrick looked like he'd been punched. Then, suddenly, he stood up straight. "No," he said firmly. "Absolutely no. I will not allow this."

As a martial artist, I'm trained to anticipate sudden physical movement. In karate, you learn to see the signs that precede an attack: the widening of the pupils, the shifting of weight, the coiling of muscle, the tightening of the shoulders. So I knew a split second before he dove, that Patrick was about to attack. I wanted to yell at him that he was too far away from Keith, that he wouldn't make it, that Keith would kill him.

But by the time anything came out of my mouth, it was too late. Patrick had lunged forward.

What surprised me, though, was that he didn't attack Keith after all. He didn't even make a run for the door. Instead, he dove across the counter, and in two strides, he'd hit his destination.

The breaker box. He was heading for the breaker box. His hand slammed down on the breaker that had been turned to the off position, the one connected to the light-bulbs in the milk jugs full of ether.

There was a sharp click, and for a moment nothing happened.

Then the world exploded into blue-white flame.

CHAPTER 20

WHEN I CAME before the Fulton County grand jury in the matter of the State of Georgia vs. Patrick Owen Triplett, III, an assistant DA named Orrin Brown asked the questions.

"Uh-huh, Ms. Childs," he was saying to me. "So did you actually *see* Patrick Owen Triplett fire the weapon?"

"No, sir, I did not."

It was a couple of weeks after Phyllis McClint was killed at the Blind Pig and I was sitting in grand jury room B, a bland, warm, woody little courtroom in the new addition to the Fulton County Courthouse. The grand jury members sat in a box off to the side. Otherwise, it was just Orrin Brown and me, plus the judge and the usual court functionaries. The grand jury consisted of ten women and three men, evenly divided between white folks and black folks. I didn't really look at them closely, but I noticed one woman was knitting and another seemed half asleep.

As I understand it, the Fulton County District Attorney devotes two of his top trial lawyers full time to murder cases, and of those two, Orrin Brown was the top dog. He was a round-faced black man with large shoulders and a bit more gut than he'd had back when he was a star runningback at Morehouse College. But he still had the restless physical energy of an athlete.

"At some point during the night Miz Childs, did you examine his table, the contents of the table, I should say?"

"Yes, I did."

"And did you find anything there?"

"Yes. I found a bullet cartridge. A spent cartridge. Meaning it had been fired already and presumably ejected from a gun."

"Where exactly was it found?"

"On the table. Sort of behind a salt shaker and the little wicker thing with the jelly in it."

"Fine. Miss Childs, did you observe anything else being found in or around the table?"

"Yes. I was there when Keith Trice found a gun next to his foot. A SIG P239."

"Okay, but returning to the cartridge found on Patrick Triplett's table. During the course of the evening, did you examine the cartridge?"

"Yes, I did. I examined the cartridge I found on Patrick's table as well as those in the gun next to his foot. I believe they were of the same caliber and the same manufacture. MagSafe nine-millimeter."

The district attorney held up a plastic bag containing six cartridge cases. "Are these the cases you examined?"

I took the bag from him. "That's right. I examined them and then put them in my pocket. After I got out of the building, I immediately turned them over to the police at the scene."

"So it sounds like you have a general acquaintance with firearms."

"Yes, I do."

"Any professional knowledge?"

I shrugged. "I'm not what you'd call a gun nut. But, sure, for professional reasons I have to have some knowledge of firearms. I've taken combat shooting classes, some GBI courses in tool mark identification and ballistics, that sort of thing."

"So based on your professional and personal knowledge, could you explain to us what happens to the bullet when a SIG P239 pistol is fired?"

"Okay, if you don't mind me getting technical for a minute, sometimes people confuse their terms when they're talking about guns. For instance sometimes people call the thing you load into a gun a bullet. But strictly speaking, it's a loaded cartridge: a brass casing full of powder with a bullet sealing the mouth of the casing. In the strict technical sense, the bullet itself is just the projectile, the slug which actually shoots out the barrel.

"So anyway, when a semiautomatic pistol such as the SIG is fired, the projectile shoots out the barrel and the brass casing is ejected from the ejector port in the slide—the slide being this steel piece that rides on the top of the barrel."

"Which direction does a SIG eject its cartridge?"

"Virtually all semiautomatic pistols eject to the right."

"Including the SIG P239 which was found under Patrick Triplett's table at the Blind Pig?"

"Including the SIG P239, yes."

"You mentioned earlier that a cartridge was found on Patrick's table. A MagSafe cartridge such as the ones you found in the pistol which was registered in his name. From Mr. Patrick Triplett's perspective, where was it found?"

"To his right."

"Uh-huh. And if Keith Trice was facing toward the back of the restaurant where Phyllis was, which direction was the cartridge with reference to him?"

"To his left."

"To his left." Orrin Brown savored the words, smiling beatifically toward the grand jury as he spoke them. Then he turned back to me. "Miss Childs, did you have occasion to interview everybody in the room during the course of the evening?"

"Yes, I did."

"And did you draw any conclusions as to who killed Phyllis McClint?"

I must have looked at Orrin Brown a little funny because he added, "Miss Childs, I'm aware that a question like that wouldn't be admissible in a trial. Since you have some experience in legal matters, you obviously find my question a little odd. However, in grand jury proceedings we are allowed a bit more latitude than we would be at trial. All we're trying to determine here is whether there is reasonable grounds for putting the question of Mr. Patrick Triplett's guilt or innocence before a jury."

"Ah," I said. "Well, to answer your question, yes, I did finally make a determination as to who I believed killed Phyllis McClint. My belief is that it was Patrick Triplett."

"Based upon what?"

"Based upon the fact that the ballistics evidence at the scene implicated him. Based on the fact that he had an apparent motive. Based on the fact that I interviewed a witness, Benny Muse, who claimed to have witnessed Patrick fire the gun. Based on evidence gathered that night by my boyfriend Barrington Cherry—who's an agent with the FBI, incidentally—indicating that Patrick had purchased the gun we found on the floor by his table. And finally based on the fact that when confronted with this evidence, he made no significant attempt to refute it. Instead he just . . . well he pretty much flipped out."

"Explain what you mean by that if you would, Miz Childs."

"Well, he attempted to flee the scene while endangering a lot of people's lives."

"I see."

"Also he confessed."

Orrin Brown's eyes widened in mock surprise. "He *confessed*?"

"Yes."

"Would it surprise you if I said that subsequently Patrick Triplett claimed to detectives that he was being sarcastic, that he was not *actually* confessing to the crime?"

I hesitated. "Well, yes. At the time it was clear he was trying to throw us off by being sarcastic. But I guess the thing was that even while being sarcastic, he managed to draw the whole crime together in a way that seemed reasonably coherent. Motive, opportunity, means. He explained it better than I could have. But to finish answering your earlier question, what finally convinced me of his guilt was what he did next. I mean, if he really didn't do it, then why did he set off the ether bombs and try to escape in the confusion?"

"Tell us about that."

"Well, as I testified earlier, Patrick jumped over the counter and set off these ether bomb devices that Keith Trice had set up. At this point, the windows and doors of the building were more or less sealed. I had actually sealed the place myself, on Keith Trice's orders.

"What I didn't mention was that while I was putting up these sheets of plywood, nailing them over the doors, Keith had given me access to a toolbox that was kept under the counter. While I was looking for nails, I also looked for a weapon, a knife or something that I could use to defend myself against Keith Trice if the occasion arose. I didn't find one. I did, however, managed to palm a small pry bar and slip it up my sleeve. The flat kind with a little hook on the end? About a foot long?

"Okay, now I'm one of these people who takes a certain amount of pride in being handy with things. I'm not some master carpenter or anything, but I can drive a nail more or less straight. But when I was hanging the plywood, I pretended that I was messing up and bending all these nails. The result was that the plywood I'd put on wasn't nailed on very firmly. There were a couple of nails that I put in straight, but I had intentionally memorized where they were so that in a pinch I could go right to the good nails, yank them out with the pry bar I'd hidden, and pull the plywood off the door.

"So anyway, what happened when Patrick set off the

burning ether was this: first, there's this huge flash. Burning ether goes flying through the air. Then, whooom, I get this weird sensation in my chest. I guess what happened was that with the plywood over the door, the ether burned all the oxygen right out of the air, at least for a few seconds. If this had happened in a well-ventilated room, we'd have probably been burned to death. But instead the flames died down a little, and then there was all this smoke and confusion.

"There was a lot of plastic in the Blind Pig, so when the ether caught fire, it also set all these plastic seat covers on fire. Immediately the room fills with black smoke. I can't breathe, I can't see. I was scared out of my mind. But I remembered what they always tell you—you know, in a fire drop to the floor and crawl, because that's where the air is.

"So as I hit the floor, I felt something dig into my side and I realized that I still had that pry bar in my pocket, the one I'd pinched from the toolbox. So I crawled over to the back door. There were a couple of people clawing at the plywood—I couldn't even make out who it was— but they weren't making any progress. And there was all this flickering ether on the floor, the smoke . . . it was a mess.

"Anyway, I tried to remember where the good nails were, then I shoved the pry bar under the plywood, popped out a couple of nails and the plywood came right off. After that somebody knocked down the door. Derl Pilgrim, I think. Then I was outside and there were police everywhere, flashing lights . . ." I closed my eyes thinking back to that strange moment. One second I thought I was going to die, the next I was free and clear.

Orrin Brown nodded, making a big show of sympathy. "That must have been a little spooky, Miss Childs."

"The whole experience was fairly unpleasant," I said dryly.

"Incidentallly, did you go back into the building?"

"Yes, I did."

"Why?"

"Well, I only saw about half the people come out. So I went back in and tried to make sure everybody was able to get out okay."

"How many times did you go back in?"

I shrugged. "A couple?"

"Must have been burning pretty good by then."

"Honestly it was hard to tell, with all the smoke. But, yeah, it was kind of toasty."

"Toasty." Orrin Brown smiled winked at me. "Miz Childs, would you hold up your arms so the jury can see?"

I held up my arms, showed off the bandages that covered them from my shoulder to the tips of my fingers. Mostly second-degree burns. I guess it could have been worse.

"Miz Childs, seems to me you're being modest. I'm going to read into the record a section of the text of a citation for bravery given to you by Mayor Bill Campbell last week." He made a show of hunting around for a paper, then came out with the silly citation that the mayor had used as an excuse to get his face on TV. "Okay, here we go. 'Whereas Sunny Childs reentered a burning building no less than three times and whereas she led several people out of the building and into safety including Mr. Benny Muse, Ms. Loretta Lynn Jones, Reverend Royce Garrick; therefore be it resolved . . .' blah blah blah. You get the point." He turned to the jury. "This young lady, folks, is a bona fide hero."

I smiled wanly. It was nice to hear, but I knew what he was doing was trying to blow my testimony up into something that sounded more conclusive than it really was. Truth was, I hadn't seen anything. Hadn't seen a gun in Patrick's hand, hadn't seen him pull the trigger.

The assistant district attorney turned to me and said, "Oh, one last question. Did you observe Patrick Triplett leaving the building?"

"Yes, I did."

"Tell us what you saw."

"Well, I was helping his wife out the door. This was the last time I went in. And Patrick was right in front of us. As soon as he came out the door, he saw something, and he—" I hesitated. It had been a confusing moment, and I wanted to be accurate in explaining what I had seen. I didn't want to make it out to be something it wasn't. "Once Patrick got out the door, he looked around. I mean, I can't say what was going through his mind, but there were police cars all around us, jammed into the alleyway behind the building. He looked around, and he sort of hesitated and then he tried to go back into the building."

"Tried?"

"By then the place was just a box full of fire. It was horrible. He tried to go back in but he couldn't. His wife screamed something at him, then he turned again and looked around. Then he just started running."

"Like he was running from the fire? Or what?"

"Maybe. There was a gap between two police cars and he headed right toward it. The cops, of course they didn't know who was a suspect and who wasn't, so a couple of them tried to tackle him. I guess he must have been a pretty good football player in his day because he just flattened this one guy, then he spun past the other one. Then here came three or four more police, a couple firemen, he's just . . ." I shrugged. "He's just running away. Just running away."

"And did they catch him?"

"Sure. He ran across the street, tried to climb the fence to the cemetery. They pulled him off the fence, knocked him down."

"Did he say anything?"

"He was just yelling. 'No, no, no, no, no!' Like that. Over and over."

"Thank you, Miz Childs." Orrin Brown smiled broadly, showing off his large square teeth. "On behalf of myself and the grand jury, thank you for you help. And thank you for your courage."

"Yeah," I said.

• • •

When I went back out into the hallway, I found a row of people sitting on benches watching me. Esther Nixon, Loretta Lynn Jones, Reverend Gerrick, Benny Muse, Bobby the grill man, plus several Atlanta PD detectives. I noticed that they hadn't bothered calling Shana Marks and Derl Pilgrim. No point putting drug dealers on the stand, I guess. Those of us who'd been in the fire all had bandages on one part or the other of our bodies. The only other person who'd been there that I didn't see was Patrick's wife, Connie.

The bailiff, a bucktoothed deputy sheriff with a gaudy ivory-handled revolver, came out and said, "Mr. Benjamin Muse."

Benny stood up uncertainly looked at me. "I'm a-scared, Miss Childs."

I smiled at him. "Don't you worry. They're nice people in there."

He smiled back and walked into the grand jury room.

I noticed one more witness arrive just as Benny walked into the room. I'd had some dealings with the Georgia Bureau of Investigation's Crime Lab over the years and so I recognized Emory Blanding, the state's expert on tool marks and firearms. We shook hands and then I sat down next to him. He was a tall, thin-faced guy who would have been handsome if it weren't for a pair of the thickest glasses I've ever seen on a man and a certain awkward, hesitant quality in his manner.

"So let me ask you a question," I said. "Did you guys recover the bullet that killed Phyllis?"

He smiled nervously. "Now, come on, Sunny. You know we're not supposed to discuss that."

"I've already testified," I said. "Won't make any difference to me."

"Then why do you want to know?"

"I want to be sure. Just for myself." I batted my eyelids

in a somewhat broad and ironic fashion. "Please? Pretty please? With sugar on top?"

Emory Blanding sighed. "There was no bullet per se. But we did find a bunch of tiny lead shot and fragments of epoxy in there."

"Mag-Safe."

"Yeah. Looks like she was killed by a MagSafe round. So there was no way to do a conventional ballistic comparison."

"Keith Trice's gun was loaded with Winchester nine-millimeters. Lead bullets. Whereas the gun found next to Patrick's table was loaded with MagSafe rounds."

"That's your testimony."

I must have looked at him kind of funny.

"We didn't recover the weapons," Emory said.

"What do you mean? Did Keith ditch the weapon before you caught him?"

Now it was Blanding's turn to look at me funny. "You didn't know?"

"Didn't know what?"

"Keith Trice was never apprehended. That's why we didn't find his gun."

"He died in the fire?"

Blanding shook his head. "No. That's what I'm saying. I mean he was never apprehended. He got away."

My eyes widened. "Five million cops standing around that building, and he *got away*?"

"I thought you would have seen on the news."

I held up my bandaged arms. "I was in the hospital for four days, drugged out of my gourd. Then I went up to the mountains for a couple of days to get away from things. Didn't watch much TV."

"Oh. Well, there was a lot of confusion. Keith Trice managed to get away in the confusion."

"You're sure he didn't get burned up?"

"Nope. No pistols and no bodies left in the fire. Got clean away."

"I'll be dog."

"They got a warrant out on him. Low-lifes like him always turn up eventually. He'll run a stop sign or get in a fight, they'll run him through the computer and that'll be that."

"I suppose."

Chapter 21

LATER THAT DAY I went out for groceries. When I got back I found a message from Esther Nixon on my box. "It occurs to me, my dear," she said, "that I never had an opportunity to explain why I needed your services. Give me a call. But please, not before noon. I can't abide being wakened before noon."

Must be nice, I thought.

Then I dialed her number.

"Ah, my dear, lovely to hear from you," Esther said. "How are you doing?"

"I'm all right. What's up?"

"Well, I realized I never really got a chance to tell you the other day why I wanted to hire you. I'm afraid it's finally happened."

"It?"

"You know, I've been a writer, a public figure of some minor note for twenty years and I've never had one. All my friends in the business have had one, but not me. But at long last I've got one."

"One *what*?" I get a little impatient when people play with me.

"A stalker!" She sounded a great deal more enthusiastic

about it than I would have. "My dear, I've finally got my own stalker, my own crazed fan."

"Do you know who it is?"

"No, I don't. I think it's a man. They've been sending red roses, love notes, making hang-up phone calls, heavy breathing, that sort of thing. Then again it might be a lesbian. Wouldn't *that* be a hoot! I'll be the envy of all the other writers at the Malice Domestic conference this year."

"You haven't had any actual contact with them, though?"

"Not yet, no."

"All right then. But this time, let's just get together at your house, huh? I'd like to bring one of my investigators to do some fingerprinting and that sort of thing. You've kept the notes and things, I trust?"

"Of *course!*"

"Good. What time can we come?"

"I write from three in the afternoon until eleven o'clock in the evening. Afterward I have a very strong gin and tonic with a twist of lime. Only then am I prepared for visitors. Say, midnight?"

"Esther, you sound like you're not taking this seriously. Stalkers are extremely dangerous people. Okay? So be careful."

"I know, I know." For the first time she sounded serious. "It's just . . . people think writers live interesting lives. They think we sit around drinking wine in cafés and having drunken conversations with fabulously witty people. We don't. Being a writer is appallingly dull. It's . . . well, I have to admit it's refreshing to have something actually *happen* in my life."

I was about to hang up, but then I thought of something. "You know, I meant to ask you: that story you were telling to Keith—you were trying to send me a message, weren't you? Without breaking Keith's little Rule One?"

"Of course, my dear! And did you receive the message?"

"You wanted me to investigate Phyllis McClint's business relationships, right? Figure out where she was getting the money to buy up all that property."

"Other than sexual perversion—which is an exception to the rule—there are only two common motives for premeditated murder," Esther said grandly.

"Greed and love."

"Correct." She sounded moderately annoyed that I had anticipated the punch line of her pronunciamento. Esther is one of those people who prefers monologue to dialogue. "Follow the money, as they say. This has none of the hallmarks of a crime of passion. It is my theory that this crime was all about money."

"It *is* your theory?" I said.

"Oh, yes. Is. I've done a bit of poking around myself. I'm quite convinced Patrick Triplett didn't kill that woman. He may be a poseur and a bad husband and third-rate literateur, but he's not a murderer."

"Then who did it?"

"What did I tell that foolish boy was the first principle of the suspense novel?"

"I forget."

"Make them wait!" She laughed airily. "See you at midnight, my dear."

"Be careful," I said.

"I'll be fine. I've bought myself a blowgun." She lowered her voice. "And some poison darts!" Then the line went dead.

Poison darts. Great. The last time she had hired us, she had developed a suspicion that her neighbor was tunneling under the fence between their properties and stealing the bulbs of her prize tulips from below ground. I had a hunch her stalker was about as silly, melodramatic, and imaginary as the tunnel had been. Or, for that matter, as her claim that Patrick wasn't the killer.

But, as they say, just because you're paranoid doesn't mean you aren't being followed.

CHAPTER 22

I WALKED OVER TO the office from my loft, sat down with my boss Gunnar Brushwood in his huge office, the mortal remains of twelve or fifteen different game animals staring dolefully down at me from the walls.

I had hoped to catch up on what had been going on at the office, but instead Gunnar leaned back in his chair, stroked his big white waxed mustache, and began to spin one of his hunting tales. Because my little run-in with fire had forced him to cut short his recent bow-hunting expedition in Montana and come back to run the shop here at Peachtree Investigations, he felt obliged to torture me with one of his endless tales of bugling elks and close shaves with death.

He had just gotten to the part where his hunting guide was suspended on the edge of a sheer rock face, the only thing keeping him from sliding down several thousand feet of rock being the string of his bow (which had caught on the root of gnarled lodgepole pine) and the indomitable will of Gunnar Brushwood (which, based upon the three thousand similar stories I had heard, could be reliably predicted to save the day), when I stood up and said, "You know, Gunnar, that is really a fascinating story, but I just remembered I have an immensely important meeting to get to."

While Gunnar gave me his usual wounded look, spluttered, and pulled on his unlit pipe, I made my escape.

There was of course no meeting, immensely important or otherwise. I love Gunnar to death, but there's something about his stories of derring-do and dead animals that sets my teeth on edge.

On the way out of the office, I stuck my head into the office of my best investigator, Tawanda Flornoy, to see if she could help me out that night. Unfortunately she was otherwise occupied, so I had to settle for the services of Earl Wickluff, who is, let's just say, *not* our best investigator.

Then I walked back to the parking garage where I keep my 1974 Eldorado, and drove down to Cabbagetown. I don't know what I was looking for, but I just felt like seeing the place where everything had happened.

The Blind Pig was utterly gone. Burned to the ground. And not just the Blind Pig. The fire must have spread, because the entire block had burned down. Previously it had been composed of a line of five or six two-story wood-frame houses all under the same roof—not quite apartments, but not quite houses either. All that was left of them was a charred patch of ground.

I parked my car on the street and got out. To my left was the street called Boulevard. On the other side of the street was the old cemetery. Rising up in front of me was the smokestack of the Fulton Bag & Cotton factory. Behind it was the mill itself, now converted into loft apartments.

I heard somebody come up behind me and clear their throat. Turning, I found myself looking at Loretta Lynn Jones, dressed in a pair of pale blue polyester slacks, a pale polyester shirt, and a scarf. Her big pile of black hair glistened with hair spray.

"You, too, huh?" she said.

"I don't know what it was," I replied. "I just kind of wanted to come down and see the place again."

"I come down here every day at five o'clock to look at it," she said. "Spent twenty-five years of my life in that dadgum place. Worked the same shift the whole time. Five to one in the morning. Now it ain't nothing left."

"What are you going to do for work? Are they building the Blind Pig back?"

She laughed bitterly. "You joking? Shoot. Some rich fellow from up in Buckhead is gonna build him a condo, take up the whole block. They say he bought him some old factory down in Newnan. He's sposeably gonna take it all down brick by brick, cart it up here, build him a fake factory, divide it up into a bunch of little bitty rooms, and then call them 'loft apartments,' sell 'em off to a bunch of dumb yuppies, probably make him a fortune. No offense."

"He must have moved awfully quick—given that the place just burned down last week."

"Turned out this fellow had what they call a option on the whole dadgum block. They'd drawed up plans over a year ago. Now that everything burned down, they's no reason not to sell the whole shebang to this fellow."

"Who owned them?"

Loretta Lynn shrugged. She didn't seem interested. The chilly wind was tugging at her big pile of hair.

"So I guess you heard that Keith Trice got away?" I said.

She nodded vaguely.

"I wonder how he did it?"

"Same way as Bobby did, most likely."

"Bobby the grill man? Through the bathroom window, you mean?"

She looked at me sharply. "Bobby didn't go out no window. If I'd of got the chance, I'd of went the same way. Only I didn't get the chance."

I looked at her curiously.

Suddenly she smiled. "I bet you don't even know what a blind pig is?"

"What, the restaurant?"

She shook her head impatiently. "You never heard of a blind pig?"

"I figured it had something to do with barbecue."

She laughed. "Back during prohibition a blind pig was another word for a speakeasy. Especially a real poor-folks type of joint. Now, if you was running an illegal gin joint, the important thing you needed was . . . what?"

"Booze?"

"Honey, you *are* out of touch."

My eyes narrowed slightly.

"Come here, hon."

I followed her as she picked her way carefully across the black ground, climbing delicately over fallen timbers and scorched brick so she wouldn't get any soot on her tiny powder blue shoes. I could see the outlines of the building in the foundations. She led me to what had been the back of the restaurant, to the L-shaped nook where the bathrooms had been.

"There," she said, pointing at the ground underneath my feet.

"What?" Under my feet lay a square slab of blackened concrete.

Loretta Lynn bent down, took a handkerchief out of her purse, scraped away at the ashes with her handkerchief. Eventually she revealed a metal handle set into a recess in the concrete.

"Yank on that, hon," she said.

I bent over, heaved on the metal handle, and the concrete slab slowly, smoothly rose up out of the ground. It was a door, well oiled and cleverly balanced so that much less force was needed to move it than its great weight would seem to require.

"Your blind pig needed a get-away hole." Loretta Lynn smiled down at me. "Case you got raided."

"Where does it come out?"

She pointed toward the cemetery. "Over there. They's a big old fancy crypt over there, the inscription on it says, ROLLIE PUCKET, REST IN PEACE, DIED OF TOO MUCH DRINKING. It was kind of a joke see. Wasn't nobody named Rollie Puckett. It's just a big marble box with a tunnel coming up inside. Back in Prohibition days, they always had somebody on the take in the police force. The cop would call up on the phone, say, 'Rollie Puckett's fixing to rise from the dead.' That meant a raid was on the way. Everybody'd duck down the hole, take the good whiskey with them. Time the raid come off, they was nothing left but two or three old drunks, and a barrel of watered-down rotgut."

I stared across the street at the cluster of headstones on the other side of the black iron fence. "Who knows about this tunnel?"

"Most folks in Cabbagetown. Old-timers like me, any-way."

"Let me ask you a question. If Keith Trice knew it was there—which he must have if he used it to get out—then how come he didn't do anything to close it up after Bobby escaped? You know how tiny that window was in the bathroom. He must have known that Bobby had gone down the hole, not out that window."

"Better question," she said, "if he knew it was there from the beginning, how come he didn't just light out down the hole as soon as the cops showed up?"

"You're right," I said. "That is a better question. Got any thoughts on the subject?"

"No ma'am."

I couldn't think of a way for it to make sense either. Not unless somebody told him about it right at the very end. But who would have done a thing like that? Maybe it was all part of Patrick's setup: let his fall guy get away so that he wouldn't talk to the police and end up saying something that might incriminate Patrick.

"What are you going to do now?" I said.

Loretta Lynn looked across the street at the graveyard.

Low, gray winter clouds moved rapidly across the sky. "It ain't the same here no more," she said. "It just ain't the same."

I drove around some more, looking at Cabbagetown, mulling things over. As I was driving, I noticed a woman walking out of a neat little house on Gaskill. I almost didn't recognize her: it was Shana. She was wearing makeup and a tailored blue suit like a secretary at a law firm might wear—nice but not expensive. She had done something to her hair. I wouldn't say it was precisely Big Hair, but it wasn't flat and lifeless anymore either. She'd cut it short, and maybe even broken out a spritz or two of hair spray.

I pulled up at the curb next to her car, a recent model Cadillac, and said, "How you doing, Shana?"

She looked at me suspiciously for a moment, then smiled brightly. "Hey, girl? You down here slumming or something?"

"Look at *you*!" I said. "You look great."

She smiled shyly.

"What's the occasion? Going down to bail somebody out of jail?" As soon as I said it, I could see I'd said the wrong thing.

The smile faded. "What the hell's that supposed to mean?"

"Hey, sorry, your line of work . . ." I shrugged. "Look I didn't mean to offend you."

There was a brief, awkward pause, then Shana said, "Nah, nah, that's all right. I'm just tetchy today."

"So what *is* the occasion?"

Shana looked at me thoughtfully for a moment, like she wasn't quite sure how to answer my question. Finally she said, "Kind of a weird experience we had the other night, huh?"

"Yeah."

"Makes you think, you know what I'm saying?"

I considered the notion for a minute and then concluded, no, that it hadn't made me think at all. Mostly I'd spent the last week trying *not* to think.

Shana smoothed the front of her suit. "Do I really look okay?"

I smiled. "Yeah. Yeah, you do."

" 'Cause I'm going to meet some people today, thinking about getting into a new line of work."

"That's probably a good plan."

I could see there was still something working around in her brain, something she was a little uncomfortable with but that she really wanted to say to me. Finally she cleared her throat. "When that ether blew up and everybody started screaming, a funny thing happened to me. I heard a voice in my head. Said, *Go forth, my child, and sin no more.*"

"Who was it?"

She squinted at me. "God," she said. Like, *what kind of moron was I?* "It was God talking to me."

"Oh. Wow."

"Yup. Went up to the church two days later. Sunday morning. Never been to church in my life. Can you believe that? Reverend Garrick says for the people who wanted to give their hearts up to Jesus to come up front, and that's what I done. Laid down on the floor and cried like a baby." She shook her head in wonderment. "You wouldn't believe the relief. Just letting all them burdens fall off my shoulders."

"I'm glad to hear it," I said.

"You wouldn't believe the things I've seen in my life. The things that's been done to me. They was just crushing me down and I didn't even know it till I felt them hands come down and lift it off of me."

"Uh-huh."

She smoothed down her jacket for the umpteenth time. "You sure I look okay?"

"Absolutely."

"I got a little money socked away, see. So I'm meeting with this man today. Kind of like a interview type of thing. Thinking about buying me a franchise business."

"That's great. What kind of franchise?"

"Check-cashing store."

Cashing checks for people too poor or ignorant to have bank accounts, charging them five bucks a transaction. I suppose it's a living. Better than selling methamphetamines to burnt-out junkies. Looking back down the hill, I could see the little houses of Cabbagetown spread out below me, then the ruined cotton mill with its high brick smokestack rising up on the far margin of the community. Through one set of eyes, it might look like any old beatdown neighborhood in America. Through another set of eyes, it probably looked like a gold mine. "Ever give any thought to real estate?" I said.

She studied my face for a moment. "*Real* estate? What I know about *real* estate, girl?"

We talked some more, long enough to go a couple minutes beyond that uncomfortable point where two people who've been through a traumatic event together realize they really have absolutely nothing in common, nothing at all to say to each other. The conversation faltered, petered out.

"Well," I said.

"Well. Yup."

"Good luck with the interview."

"Yup. Yup. You too."

I got in my old Eldorado and started up the engine. As I was about to pull away from the curb, Shana signaled for me to roll down the window.

"Hey, that crazy writer lady—she a friend of yours?"

"Sort of."

"I heard she was going around asking a bunch of questions about what happened the other day. Saying how it wasn't Patrick Triplett that done it."

"Oh?"

Shana squinted at me. "I'm trying to think how to say this . . ."

"Just say it."

"This ain't Buckhead. You know? Folks go around asking questions, they liable to get some hurt put on them."

"I thought you got saved and all," I said harshly.

"I did."

"Then why are you suddenly making threats?"

"Threats? Shit! That's *why* I'm telling you. Trying to be a good Christian, that's all."

I kept looking at her.

She leaned in the window, lowered her husky voice a little. "They's stuff hid under rocks around here. Maybe got nothing to do with what happened to you and me the other night. So I'm just saying. Ain't no profit in getting all up in nobody's business. Not in Cabbagetown."

CHAPTER 23

ONE OF THE annoyances of being a private detective is that you're always getting collect calls from prisoners. If you're dumb enough to actually take the call, the prisoner will invariably give you a long, rambling hard-luck story about his "situation" (it's never a "crime," it's a "situation") and finally wind up by asking you to investigate his "situation" so that you can prove his innocence. And, equally invariably, he wants you to do this for free. Because he's innocent, right?

Out of guilt or boredom, I'd dropped by the office after going down to Cabbagetown. It was around six when the phone rang. My assistant had gone home by then, so I answered the phone call myself.

A computerized voice on the other end of the line told me I was about to receive a collect call from the Fulton County Jail. I was about to hang up when the computer told me the caller's name.

After a long pause, I said, "What is it, Patrick?"

"I'll make this quick," Patrick Triplett said. "Put aside the forensic stuff, this whole case comes down to one thing. The word of a moron with an IQ of twenty-five."

"And?"

"Somebody got to him. Somebody paid him or threatened him or something. Because there was never a gun in my hand and I never shot that woman."

"And?"

"So I want to hire you. I want you to find out who leaned on that goddamn retard."

I laughed as unpleasantly as I could manage.

"Seriously. I'm not holding it against you that you testified against me."

"It kind of puts me in a conflict of interest situation, don't you think?"

"No it doesn't. If you find out I'm innocent, great. If not, then you can tell a jury, 'Hey, I took this guy's money and I *still* think he did it.' "

"It's not a good idea."

"Look, Sunny, here's the deal. That friend of yours, the writer? She was more or less on the money about my background. Dull prosperous South Georgia family."

"And?"

"Look, point is, my daddy owns about half of Troup County. He's willing to do whatever it takes to get me off the hook here. Money no object."

"I said no."

"Sunny, Sunny, hold on. Seriously, I was impressed with your performance that night. Whatever your usual rate is, Daddy will triple it."

"Oh, I get it. You want to buy me off, get me to change my testimony."

"Give me some credit here. I can tell you're not the type to go for something like that."

"What type am I?"

"The competent type."

"Not that I don't enjoy flattery, but the answer's still no."

I hung up.

Truth is, I didn't turn the guy down because I thought there was a conflict of interest. I turned him down because Gunnar and I have the luxury these days of turning down business we don't like. And putting aside the fact that Patrick Triplett was a murderer, I just didn't like the guy.

CHAPTER 24

I PICKED UP Earl Wickluff at his apartment complex. He's about fifty years old, divorced three times, and lives in one of these apartment complexes that's largely populated—as far as I can tell—by sorority-girl types with low-level white collar jobs and perky breasts. On his off days during the summers Earl can always be found out by the pool, drinking Carling Black Label and wearing mirrored shades so he can stare at all the smooth-bottomed cuties in their thong bathing suits. Since it was winter and eleven-thirty at night, however Earl was holed up inside his apartment, watching pornos.

He made a point of leaving the tape of a couple of moaning lesbians running while he gathered his mountain of surveillance gear.

"Got the thermal imaging," he said. Earl's one of these guys who is under the misapprehension that fancy equipment makes a good investigator. "That new Russian military surplus model I was telling you about. Fingerprint kit. Wireless unidirectional mic. Four-hundred-millimeter lens on the Nikon . . ."

"What do we need a four-hundred-millimeter lens for, Earl?" I said. "We're not doing a stakeout. We're just going over to talk to a kooky old lady."

"I was an Eagle Scout, babe." He insists on calling me babe, despite the fact I'm his boss. I would have fired him years ago, except that Gunnar likes him because he laughs at all his jokes. "Be prepared. That's the Earl Wickluff motto."

"I'm glad to hear it. Have you got a pen and some paper?"

He looked around furtively. "Hm, gosh, you know . . ."

He brings the thermal imaging equipment, but forgets to bring a pen. That's Earl in a nutshell.

We got to Esther Nixon's house at a few minutes before midnight. She lives in a modest bungalow in Virginia Highlands that she bought for cash with royalties from the only book she's written that hit the bestseller list. This would have been back before the real-estate prices went through the roof in that neighborhood.

The lights were on in the front room, but the curtains were down. I pulled in and Earl started struggling with his black boxes full of investigator chic.

"Leave the gear, Earl," I said. "You can come out for it later if you need it."

Earl grunted. "This client, she an attractive woman?"

"Depends what you like, I guess."

"Young and frisky, that's how I like 'em."

I knocked on the door. "Oh, Earl? Do me another favor, would you? Since you're such an Eagle Scout, pretend I'm the scoutmaster, okay? That means, don't talk until I tell you to. Esther is a kind of self-dramatizing woman. This whole stalker thing may be some sort of invention she's dreamed up to liven up her life. So if it turns out that's the case, don't make a big deal about it, okay? Just smile and do what I say."

Earl sighed wearily. He considers himself a sort of Job-like figure for having been cursed with a young woman as a boss. Maybe he'd have suffered me a little more gladly if I had large perky breasts.

I knocked on the door again. When there was no immediate answer I rang the doorbell three or four times for good measure. I know that sort of thing annoys people, but I get impatient easily.

Still no answer.

I knocked a third time. No answer.

"Maybe she's on the throne."

"Thank you, Earl, for that tasteful and helpful thought. Go around, would you, check the back door."

He winked at me, pulled the headgear for his thermal imaging goodie out of the capacious pocket of his trench coat, slipped it over his head. He now looked like the bad guy in some Wes Craven slasher flick, blank reflective sensors poking out of his face where his eyes should have been. "Never can be too careful, babe," he said. "Could be unfriendlies back there."

"Go." I kept my voice amazingly level, all things considered.

Earl Wickluff disappeared into the bushes at the side of the house.

I'm not big on guns. But I'm not afraid of them either. When a client says they're being threatened by a crazy person, I make a point to take the threat seriously. I pulled out my sidearm of choice, a short-barreled Smith & Wesson .38 revolver, and knocked on the door one more time, this time harder.

Just when I was starting to get nervous, the door opened and there was Esther Nixon wearing one of her usual garish but shapeless dresses, a very large drink in her hand.

"My dear, thank God!" she said. "You're just in time!"

"Oh?"

"There's a strange man standing on my back porch. He's wearing some sort of thing on his head like that creepy fellow wore in the last scene of *Silence of the Lambs*."

"It's okay. That's Earl Wickluff. He works for me."

Esther looked vaguely disappointed. "Oh." She paused,

then looked perplexed. "Why is he skulking around on my back porch?"

"When you didn't answer the door, I got worried."

"Well. That's too bad. I thought we were going to have some sort of excitement. Do come in." She raised her eyebrows. "I had the blowgun ready!"

I followed her into the house, which was crammed with stuff. Furniture, paintings, sculpture, African masks, folk art, pottery, books, and a wonderful jumble of beautiful furniture, none of which even vaguely matched. She had a massive Thornton Dial painting hanging on the wall of her living room. Dial is one of the few authentic folk artists I know of whose work particularly interests me. It was a huge tiger, jaws gaping, painted with great slashes of yellow paint. The eyes burned with an opaque, inhuman hunger.

"I better go get my operative," I said. "Before he shoots somebody by accident."

I poked my head out the back door. "Earl? Hey, Earl!"

No answer.

"Earl!"

I didn't know whether to get irritated or worried. Knowing Earl, he'd probably seen a mole or a possum through his high-tech vision system and decided to track it through the neighborhood. Then again, maybe he'd gone back around front. I closed the door, locked it, went back out front.

Earl came charging around the corner, out of breath.

"I lost him!" he gasped.

"Lost who?"

"There was some guy in the yard!"

"Where in the yard?" I asked sharply.

"In the back. By the tree line at the far end of the property. Of course as soon as I came around the side of the house, I saw him. His heat signature stuck out like a sore thumb. I headed toward him and he hauled ass. Good thing I was wearing this system, huh? Never would of seen him without it."

"Yeah," I said. I looked up and down the street. There was no one skulking in the bushes, as best as I could tell. "Can you give me a description?"

"He looked green and orange." Earl smiled condescendingly.

"Seriously. What did the guy look like?"

"Infrared only senses heat, Sunny. It ain't much for making out facial features. It was a short guy. Or maybe a woman. Hard to tell."

"Okay. Let's go inside."

We went into Esther's house and Earl plopped down under the Thornton Dial painting.

"Love your work, Miz Nixon," Earl said unctuously. This from a guy who probably hadn't read the back of a cereal box—much less a book—in twenty years.

"Before you get too comfortable, Earl," I said, "do me a favor. Go back where you saw this guy and see if you can find any shoe prints. Be nice if we could get a plaster cast of a shoe print." I turned to Esther. "It looks like this has gotten fairly serious. Earl saw someone on your property."

Esther blinked. "Oh, I wouldn't worry about that. Probably just Mr. Corcoran down the street. He's a Peeping Tom. Watches me through my windows whenever I change clothes."

"Uh . . . How come you don't close your shades?"

"Well, naturally, the thought has crossed my mind." She batted her eyelids. "But for a woman of my age, it's terribly flattering. I mean, he's not *dangerous* or anything."

This is the kind of thing that gives people gray hair in the personal protection business: half your clients turn out to be their own worst enemies. It's just one of several reasons why I steer our firm away from bodyguard work. "Well, we should check it out anyway."

After Earl left, I said, "So let's get down to it. Tell me about what's led you to believe someone is stalking you."

"There have been several notes, full of the most appalling sexual innuendo. I'll show them to you later. I think we're dealing with some sort of sexual deviant. He's also sent flowers." She pointed to a vase full of red roses sitting on a table at my elbow. Among the flowers was a cream-colored envelope.

I pulled on a pair of surgical gloves and took the card out of the envelope. The message was printed by a dot matrix printer on a card with the logo of a nearby flower shop at the top. The message said, *Let's make beautiful love, my sweetest flower.*

"Probably won't get any fingerprints off it," I said. "But it's worth a try. Most likely they called in the order and the flower shop printed it on their own printer."

"Oh, well, do whatever seems necessary. But it's not terribly interesting to me at the moment," Esther said. "I'm far more interested in this Patrick Triplett person."

I had had a hunch all along that that was where this was leading.

"Before you get started on that," I said, "I want you to remember that I've got an operative fooling around in your back yard who's running you sixty-five bucks an hour. And I'm costing you a good deal more than that. So I'm happy to talk about anything you want. But I don't want you to get some kind of nasty surprise when I send you the bill."

"I'm a selfish old woman with plenty of money and no heirs. Indulge me."

"Consider yourself indulged."

Esther sat for a moment as though collecting herself. "This young man, Patrick Triplett—don't people like him fascinate you?"

"He's a spoiled ex-jock from East Jesus County who came to the big city thinking he was going to be God's gift to literature. Somebody got in the way of his little dream and he killed them. So, no, I guess people like him don't really fascinate me. Mostly they piss me off."

She pressed one finger against her lip. Her nails were long and painted a lurid red, but the nail polish was chipping badly. "Did I tell you on the phone that he didn't do it?"

"You told me that you *thought* he didn't do it."

"Well, I've been asking some questions around Cabbagetown. Hard questions." She leaned toward me, raised her eyebrows melodramatically. "*Probing* questions."

"No kidding. What did you find out?" I knew there was no point in asking, though. The quality that makes Esther so amusing is the same quality that makes her so infuriating: she's utterly self-dramatizing. And, as she said at the Blind Pig that night, the first principle of drama is making you wait. God forbid she just come right out and tell me something. She was probably going to spend the rest of the night dangling hints and beating around the bush, before triumphantly whipping out whatever "evidence" she'd turned up.

"I have *clues*," she said in her most confidential and portentous tone of voice.

"Somehow I had a hunch," I said dryly.

I was making a note to myself to give some consideration to moving her from our Schedule N billing list—the amusing clients for whom we lower our fees—and putting her on the Schedule A list reserved for high-ticket pains-in-the-ass. She had always been hovering there on the border between the two. But when she was stringing me along after I'd stayed up just to meet with her at this late and inconvenient hour, Schedule A was looking more and more appropriate.

"Remember when we were in the Blind Pig, I implied through the medium of my little tale that one ought to find out from whence Phyllis McClint received her investment funds?"

"Sure."

"I went to several rather grim nursing homes and interviewed various elderly people who had sold their homes to Phyllis in the past several years. Some of them showed me their sales contracts. What I discovered is that, although they all told me that they had sold to Phyllis personally, the sales contracts were in the names of something called Blind Pig Enterprises, Ltd. I then went down to the County Courthouse and looked at the plat books for Cabbagetown. Did you know that over one-third of the property in Cabbagetown either is or was owned by Blind Pig Enterprises? A shell company, obviously."

"So who owns Blind Pig Enterprises?"

"Funny you should ask. I spent a few hours in the Georgia Secretary of State's office. Terribly nice people there—much more polite than the ladies working for Fulton County, I must say. To make a short story long, it's rather difficult to uncover the true ownership of a limited partnership in the state of Georgia. One can, however, find out the officers of the corporation."

"Okay."

"The managing partner was Phyllis McClint. The attorney of record, one Delbert Rathrock."

"Let me guess, you went to talk to this Dilbert guy."

"*Del*bert. With an E. Rathrock." Esther smiled. "Indeed I did talk to him."

"And he told you, 'I can't disclose the names of clients, blah blah blah.' "

"He wasn't that polite. But yes, that was the gist of it. In the course of my visit, however, I discovered something terribly terribly *terribly* interesting." She paused expectantly. "Would you like to see?"

"Sure," I said. "I'd love to know where this is heading."

"You just wait right here, my dear. I'll go get it."

She walked out of the room, her Chinese house slippers slapping on the floor as she disappeared into the next room. After a moment, I heard the back door open, then the house was silent for a while.

"Goodness, goodness gracious." Esther's voice floated through the house, then I heard a thump and a shuffling sound, as though she were moving a box or some other heavy object.

Then the house was silent again.

I looked at the Thornton Dial tiger, then at some other

pieces of art on the walls—a cheap reproduction of a muscular Diego Rivera peasant, a lovely Kathe Kolwitz print of a sad old woman, and what sure as hell looked like an original Picasso, a drawing of a busty woman with a flower in her hat.

After a while it occurred to me that Esther was taking an awfully long time coming back with her "clues." Knowing her flair for drama, I would have expected her to have whatever "evidence" she'd collected close at hand so she could bringing it out with the proper flourish.

"Esther?"

The house was silent. Suddenly I got a nervous feeling, and I noticed that the temperature in the room had dropped a few degrees

"Esther? You okay?"

No answer. I'd heard the back door open; maybe she had gone outside.

I walked into the kitchen, found the door to the back porch was wide open, the cold night air flooding into the room. I looked outside. The door was unlocked, so I just pushed it open and stuck my head out. "Esther? Earl? Anybody?"

The yard was dark, silent, the air cold. Nothing moved.

If it had been a movie, this would have been a point where the creepy discordant violin music would have started rising in the background.

"Earl? Where are you?"

That was when I saw him. He was lying on the ground about twenty feet away. I pulled out my Smith for the second time that night, then ran across the yard.

As I approached him, Earl sat up slowly. "I'm okay, I'm okay," he said. There was blood on his face.

I grabbed him by the sleeve and dragged him to his feet. His eyes were unfocused, childlike. "Move!" I shouted.

Then I pulled him back toward the house. Inside, he collapsed onto a chair. There was a long, nasty gash across his forehead that was bleeding profusely.

"What happened?"

He looked at me dully. "I'm okay," he said. "I'm just a little shook up."

"What the hell happened?"

He shrugged vaguely. "I didn't see. It just . . . rose up out of the ground. Boom."

There was no time to cajole a more understandable story out of him. Gun straight out in front of me in a two-hand carry, ready to shoot, I worked my way slowly through the house. If you've ever been in a situation where you may have to confront or even kill somebody, somebody who may be inclined to kill you—well, it's not like anything else I've ever experienced. My limbs were tingling, my vision had narrowed, and there was a field of odd hissing in my ears that blotted out all the rest of the sounds in the house.

As it turned out, though, there was no one to confront, no one to shoot at. By the time I had reached the back bedroom, there was nothing else to be done.

Esther Nixon lay sprawled on the floor, her misshapen head covered with blood, the tip of her tongue poking out of her mouth in way that would have been cheeky if she'd been alive. But in a dead woman, it was sickening. On the floor next to her corpse lay a blood-slick crowbar.

So much for self-dramatization.

Chapter 25

F OR ME THERE had been something vaguely surreal about the whole experience in the Blind Pig. It was horrible of course, but I didn't know Phyllis McClint, and in the course of the event I'd managed to get some control over the situation in a way that had made it easier to handle psychologically. But Esther Nixon's murder was different. Not only was she a friend, but her death had been my failure.

I made it through the initial conversations with the cops at the crime scene, but then they brought me back to the station. It was three o'clock in the morning by then, and the homicide detective in charge of the case took me back to his office, a cubicle, and sat me down.

I had dealt with the detective once before, a guy named Major Carl Fontaine. He was a man I trusted. Fontaine was a mildly dopey looking, badly dressed black guy—the only guy in the Atlanta Police Department homicide squad who didn't dress like a banker—but I knew him to be exceptionally bright, determined, and decent. He asked me to go over everything again.

I told him about how I'd been hired by Esther to investigate the stalker, about how I hadn't taken my assignment too seriously.

"Well, you didn't really have a chance to get started on it," Fontaine said.

I know he meant it kindly, that he meant I could hardly blame myself for blowing an assignment that had only lasted ten minutes. But it seemed humorous to me for some reason, humorous in a nasty way. And that, at long last, was when I lost it. I started laughing. I started laughing and I kept laughing until I literally fell off my chair onto the floor, where I lay in a fetal ball. It was that hysterical kind of laughter that eventually turns into crying. I kept laughing until the muscles in my stomach were on fire and my throat was burning and then somewhere along the way I started crying and I couldn't stop.

I don't mean I couldn't stop for a while, I mean I couldn't stop, *period*. I cried and cried and cried, lying on the floor in a ball. After a while Major Fontaine got a worried look on his face, and still I was crying, and so he called Barrington, and Barrington came over and picked me up and still I was crying and we went home and still I was crying. And it wasn't that weepy, dab-the-eyes-with-tissue sort of thing: I'm talking about gulping, gasping, sobbing, wracking groans. We went back home, and I kept crying and crying and finally Barrington took me to the emergency room at Grady and a nice, over-worked Pakistani doctor came out and gave me a shot, and after that I don't remember much of anything.

So I lay around the house for about a week, taking tranquilizers and painkillers—painkillers because somehow in all that hysterical crying I had managed to crack one of my ribs—and sleeping pills, drinking cheap wine, and watching the parade of jerks and cretins that passes for entertainment on TV these days. The world seemed gauzed in ugliness and decay, and all the foul dreck I saw on TV only confirmed it. The Bangladeshis were washing away again, a couple of whacked-out kids had opened fire on their friends at a Bible camp in Ohio, midgets and lesbians and hookers were calling each other names on

various talk shows, beautiful young women were humil-
iating themselves in all sorts of ways in order to get parts
in Hollywood, boys with nose rings were smashing their
guitars, loud-voiced men were selling juicers to credulous
people who thought carrot juice would keep them from
dying. It went on and on, and I just sat there absorbing
it, feeling like I was lying under four feet of wet, reeking
slime.

On the following Monday Barrington said to me, "No
joke, baby, you need to see somebody."

"I'll be fine," I said. "Just give me a couple days."

"No, you need to see somebody. Now."

"It's just the painkillers," I said. "My rib still hurts like
hell, and the codeine's making me a little woozy. Really.
I'll be fine."

Barrington scowled but let it go.

Saturday rolled around and I was still sitting around the
house in my black pajamas. Around noon I went to the
refrigerator to pour my third glass of wine for the day,
and I found that my box of Gallo Hearty Burgundy had
run dry.

I put a coat over my pajamas, pulled on a pair of Tony
Lamas, went down to the street, and walked three blocks
down to the liquor store over on Marietta. It was the kind
of place that only bums go to, with a Lotto terminal, a
full rack of Night Train and MD-20/20, plus an encyclo-
pedic collection of malt liquors and porn magazines. I had
to stand in line behind four scruffy, stinking, beat-down
men, each clutching a bottle of fortified wine while en-
viously eyeing a prostitute in a rabbit skin coat, who was
flush enough to spring for a large bottle of Mr. Boston
Vodka.

The guy at the front of the line was scrabbling around
in his pockets, trying to find enough change to pay for
his can of St. Ives malt liquor. I suspect he was short, just
trying to scam the store owner. But the owner, a big tough

Korean guy had been scammed by one wino too many and wasn't having it.

"Next!" the store owner said. "Who next?"

"Yo, man, I'm trying to—"

"Next! Next!"

The wino started acting aggressive and it was looking to turn into some kind of desperate shoving match.

I opened my purse to get a buck for the bum—anything to get at my third glass of wine—and as I pull out my wallet, I noticed something, something that I'd completely forgotten about. A three-by-four-inch card with a message printed on it that said, *Let's make beautiful love, my sweetest flower.*

I don't know why, but something about it struck me as phony—though I'd be hard-pressed to say exactly what it was. I kept staring at the card until suddenly I noticed I was standing at the register, the Korean guy glaring at me as I clutched my plastic box of Gallo wine.

"You want?" he said. "You want or you not want? People in line!"

I set the wine box on the counter. "Not, I believe."

CHAPTER 26

RIKKI'S FLOWERS WAS on Peachtree at the south end of Buckhead about four or five blocks from where Esther lived. It was a hole-in-the-wall store, a leftover from the days before the area had been completely overwhelmed by places that sold four-dollar cups of coffee or six-dollar loaves of bread or single-malt scotch at twelve bucks to the glass. The owner was an old lady with blue-rinsed beauty parlor hair, a sweater with a pink cat appliqued on it, and half moon-shaped glasses that hung on a chain around her neck.

I breezed in the door and told her I was a detective, that I was investigating a murder. Then I showed her the card from Esther's flowers, the ones that had been sent by her stalker.

"What I need you to do is pull the credit card receipt for this sale."

The old lady looked at me skeptically. I was still wearing my nappy black Viet Cong-looking pajamas and my ratty black trench coat.

I smiled curtly. "Working undercover."

She pushed her lips together skeptically. "I believe I might need to see some identification, ma'am."

I took out my sheriff's reserve deputy badge—something I received some years back after Gunnar dragooned me into contributing four hundred bucks to a former sheriff's political campaign—and flashed it briefly.

"Is that real?" the old lady said. "That looks like plastic."

Had I been slightly more sober, I might not have done what I did next. But I wasn't. I had two glasses of wine in me, and a cute little blue pill that I think was codeine but that might have been something else.

I simply climbed over the counter, pulled the keyboard of the old lady's computer out and started punching things in. It had a simple menu, and looked like it wouldn't be hard to figure out.

The old lady whacked me several times with a newspaper, but with the codeine in me it didn't even hurt. She eventually gave up and just stood there while I messed around.

"Oh for pity's sake," she said finally. "Let *me* do it."

I moved over and she tapped a few keys and the name of the person who had ordered and paid for Esther Nixon's flowers came up on the screen.

"That's who *ordered* them?" I said dubiously.

"Yes ma'am. Ordered and paid." She bent over, pulled out a pile of receipts from a box under the counter, leafed through them until she found the actual credit card imprint. "See?"

The name of person who ordered the flowers was the same as the name on the credit card receipt. It blinked at me from the screen. ESTHER NIXON.

CHAPTER 27

I COULDN'T REACH Major Fontaine, the homicide detective, to tell him that the stalker theory was out the window, that it had just been a goof Esther had dreamed up for her own amusement. I left a message for him to call me, then went to bed and slept most of the day.

When I got up, it was about three in the afternoon. I tried Fontaine again, but he was out of the office. I checked my machine, found that he had left a message returning my call. Apparently in my codeine-induced sleep, I hadn't heard the phone ring. The good news was that the codeine was more or less out of my system. The rib I'd broken during my hysterical fit hurt every time I breathed—but there was something comforting about that. It made me feel alive again.

I took a shower for the first time in several days and then got dressed, trying to think who might have had reason to kill Esther. It pretty much came down to this: if she had invented the stalker, then she must have been right when she claimed that Patrick Triplett was innocent. She must have gone down there to Cabbagetown and figured something out.

I tried to think back to what she'd said about the case.

People killed for one of two reasons. Love or money. She said this was about money, about who owned what property down there in Cabbagetown. I looked at my watch. It was four-fifteen. The courthouse closed in forty-five minutes.

I ran out the door and jogged all the way to the courthouse, arriving out of breath as the stream of county workers headed out the door, trying to beat the weekend traffic.

I took the escalator up to the second floor, where the registry of deeds is, charged in the door, asked the lone clerk at the long counter to see the plat book for Cabbagetown.

The clerk, who sat on a tall stool behind a layer of bulletproof glass, was a beautifully dressed black man with a shiny bald head and fringe of salt-and-pepper hair over his ears. A small plastic sign at his elbow said MR. PIPLEY. He was bent over a book. He didn't look up at me, just kept reading.

I put my mouth close to the vent hole in the bulletproof glass and loudly repeated my request.

Mr. Pipley sighed slowly but inaudibly, his shoulders falling in slow motion, as though my request was not merely crushing the life out of him, but was inexorably destroying his immortal soul. He still didn't look up from his book.

"Madam," he said finally, still without looking up from his book, "the Fulton County Registry of Deeds closes in ten minutes."

"I'll be done in five. All I need is the plat book for Cabbagetown."

Another long, torpid sigh. Mr. Pipley reached under the counter, came up—slowly! slowly!—with a tooled leather bookmark which he placed, just so, in his book. He then closed the book carefully, ran his finger along the binding as though to make certain it had sustained no damage during its recent workout, then finally looked up at me.

He raised his eyebrows as though puzzled to find me still standing there.

"The plat book?" I said loudly. "For Cabbagetown?"

Mr. Pipley's left eyebrow rose a fraction of an inch, and the lids of both his eyes drooped slightly. "Madam," he said. "I can only retrieve a plat book for you by plat number."

"Okay. Well, how do I find out the plat number for Cabbagetown?"

The life-crushing, soul-destroying sigh again. Mr. Pipley lifted his finger slowly, as though at great cost to his small stock of energy, and pointed at something.

"What?" I said irritably. "What are you pointing at?"

But he said nothing, just continued to point. Then, having apparently invested sufficient energy in my predicament, he looked down at the book again—it was entitled *Pray . . . and Get Rich!*—slowly opened the book, ran one long finger down the seam between the two pages, and began to read again.

"Sir? Sir? Excuse me?"

But it was hopeless. He wouldn't be roused.

I went across the room to where he was pointing, found a master plat map that broke the city down into plat sections. Cabbagetown was split into two sections. With a Bic pen I wrote down the volume numbers for both plat books on the back of my hand, then went over to the counter again.

"Sir. I hate to bestir you from your labors again, but I'd like to get these two plat books." I held out the palm of my hand with the two numbers written on it.

Mr. Pipley continued to read for a while, then finally looked up, pointed to a small hand-lettered sign that said, ALL PLAT BOOK REQUESTS MUST BE MADE IN WRITING ON *THIS FORM*!!!!! There was an arrow scrawled next to the sign which pointed down to a small plastic bin the size of an in-box. The bin was empty.

"There's no form," I said.

Mr. Pipley went through his ritual again: the sigh, the

search for the leather bookmark, the closing of the book, the tactile examination of the binding. Without saying anything to me he walked back through a door and disappeared.

It was two minutes till 5:00 by the time he came back. In his hand he had a single piece of paper which he set down on the counter, then pushed it toward me through a steel slot, one finger on each of the two corners closest to him.

I filled out the piece of paper with my name and the two plat books I wanted, pushed it back through the slot.

He looked at the paper uncomprehendingly and didn't move.

"Is there a problem?" I said after a very long period of time had passed.

He pressed the paper against the glass and pointed to the bottom of the form, where it said in letters so tiny as to be barely legible, "Only one request per form."

"Okay," I said, "just give me G-41."

He set the form down, took a gold pen out of his pocket, took the lid off with a certain amount of decorousness and care, scribed a thin blue line through G-42, then turned and called out, "Mrs. Fredricks? G-41, if you would be so kind."

Then out came the book about how to use God to get rich.

Eventually a fat, shiftless-looking white woman came out with a plat book which she tossed on the counter next to Mr. Pipley. She then shuffled away. Mr. Pipley continued to stare at his book.

"Sir?" I said. "Mr. Pipley?"

He looked up at me as though once again deeply surprised by my continuing presence.

"Sir? The book?"

He looked at me, then at the plat book. Then he reached up and slid a sign into a slot on the bulletproof glass. CLOSED.

"Oh come *on!*"

Mr. Pipley pointed at the clock. It was five on the nose.

"You know something," I said, pointing at *Pray . . . and Get Rich!* "I read that one, too. In fact, I'm going to pray for you to get rich right this minute."

Mr. Pipley looked up at me disinterestedly. I put my hands together and rolled my eyes piously toward the ceiling, doing my best imitation of one of those saints in a medieval altar painting. When I was done, I opened my purse and took out two twenties and a ten. I set the money down in the slot.

"Yeah, the Big Guy just spoke to me," I said. "He told me you could make an easy fifty bucks if you give me the plat books. Both of them."

"Praise the Lord," Mr. Pipley said. The money disappeared into Mr. Pipley's pocket with startling rapidity.

Five minutes later I knew who Phyllis McClint's partner was in every single building she'd owned. Twenty-two properties in all, and according to the plat books, they were all owned outright by Blind Pig Enterprises. But there was also a mortgage lien listed on each property and it was held by the same company: an outfit called Cabco Financial Corp.

CHAPTER 28

ACCORDING TO THE phone book, Cabco Financial was located at 3121 Howell Mill Road. I drove up Northside Drive, cut over onto Howell Mill, and eventually found the place. It was a concrete bunker of a building, mostly lawyers' and dentists' offices, which had probably been "modern" looking about forty years ago, but which now looked like an abandoned military fortification. If I were to guess, the lawyers were mostly third-rank ambulance chasers and the dentists were the kind who subsisted in large part on insurance fraud.

A directory in the lobby listed Cabco as having offices on the third floor. The elevator made a hellish shrieking noise when I pushed the button so I decided to take the stairs.

Glued to a long frosted glass window beside the door of the office at the far end of the dimly lit third floor hall was a cheap engraved plastic sign. At the top in large letters the sign said DELBERT RATHROCK, ATTORNEY/ABOGADO. The name rang a bell, but I couldn't quite remember why. Then below that in smaller letters was a list of six or seven bogus-sounding companies, the last of which was Cabco Financial.

I was considering what to do next when I saw some-

thing moving behind the frosted glass, a person who
seemed to be fumbling with a briefcase or something. I
decided to back off and see who came out.

There was a ladies' room hálfway down the hallway.
There was a lock on the door, but the hasp was bent, so
I was able to push it open. I went in and peered through
the crack. At the far end of the hallway, the door to Delbert Rathrock's office opened and a skinny woman with
frizzy red hair came out. She walked down to the elevator,
got in and disappeared. As soon as she was gone, the light
in the office went out and a short chubby man came out.
He wore a tan silk suit with four buttons, brown-on-tan
saddle shoes, a very long mohair coat, and a tan homburg.
A large paisley handkerchief erupted foppishly from his
breast pocket, and his hair lofted up and back from his
brow in full televangelical splendor. There was an aggressive, almost wolfish quality to his face. The only thing
that seemed incongruous about him was that instead of a
briefcase, he carried a cheap backpack like a highschool
girl might carry her books in.

I watched him hustle to the elevator, where he proceeded to stab at the down button with a short broad finger
until the doors finally opened. He got in and the doors
closed.

There was something vaguely familiar about the guy,
but I couldn't place it. Maybe he was one of those guys
that advertised his law practice on Channel 69 at three
o'clock in the morning. *Car wreck? Injured on the job?
Call Delbert Rathrock and get the cash you deserve!*—
that kind of thing. Or maybe not. The little guy was like
an afterimage burned on your retina—the same as the real
thing but different colors . . . and all of it fading away, no
matter how hard you squeezed your eyes shut.

Sometimes when you're an investigator, you just flat
don't know what to do. Not only do you not know what
to do, but you feel like somebody else—somebody better
trained and smarter, a *real* private investigator—*would*
know what to do. Should I have just walked up to the

foppish little fat guy—I assumed he was Delbert Rathrock—and asked him what Cabco Financial was, who owned it, where the money came from? No, because he would have given me the same rude blow-off speech he gave Esther. *Client confidentiality, yadda yadda, get your skinny butt out of my office.* Should I have followed him? Maybe. But what good would it do to find out where he lived or what kind of car he drove? If I'd been a PI on television, I'd have taken out my lock pick collection and broken into the office—but not only do I not know how to pick locks or defeat alarm systems, but breaking into places is illegal and stupid and dangerous, and you can get sent to jail and lose your PI license for doing it.

So that left me right where I'd started: crouched in the corner of a bathroom that smelled oppressively of fake lilacs and urine, peeping through a crack in a door, and feeling like an aimless loser and amateur.

I walked back down to the door, read the crummy plastic sign.

DELBERT RATHROCK, ATTORNEY/ABOGADO

CRB, LTD.

GOLDTONE, INC.

HI-FIVE FEATURED PRODUCTS, INC.

NNNB, INC.

PHALANX REAL PROPERTIES, LTD.

INTERNATIONAL CHECK CASHING CORP.

CABCO FINANCIAL, LTD.

My eye froze on the next-to-last line. International Check Cashing. "Oh my God," I said.

I picked up my phone and called Major Carl Fontaine. This time he was in.

"Meet me at 212 Horton Street," I said.

"Who lives there?"

"Her name's Shana Marks."

"Who's that?"

"I'll explain later."

CHAPTER 29

WHEN WE GOT to Shana's house, the little building was at a full blaze, the flames licking up into the darkening sky, lighting up the faces of the crowd of onlookers. Among them were several faces I recognized. Loretta Lynn, Benny, Bobby, and all four of the old people who'd been inside the Blind Pig. Plus a lot more besides.

"Did Shana get out?" I said to Loretta Lynn.

She looked at me for a moment with an oddly amused expression. "*Oh* yeah. She got out, believe you me."

I guess I must have looked perplexed.

"She left town," Loretta Lynn said.

"When?"

Loretta Lynn shrugged. "Two, three days ago. Pulled up a U-Haul truck, couple big strong boys tuck her things out, she drove away. Didn't say boo to nobody." She looked oddly wistful. "Her hair looked real pretty, though."

"I thought she was going to start up some kind of business. Check cashing or something."

Loretta Lynn shrugged disinterestedly. "I heard that didn't pan out."

"So how did the place burn up?"

"You know how it is. Soon as somebody moves out,

the crackheads move in. Reckon one of them dropped a match, set the place on fire."

The roof caved in just as the fire trucks rolled up and the sky filled with sparks. Carl Fontaine arrived just behind the trucks.

"What was this all about?" the detective asked me.

The firemen were rushing around, spraying the wreck of a building, but it was all beside the point. There was nothing left by then.

"I don't know," I said. "I thought it was her, but maybe I was wrong." Then I explained about the flowers that Esther Nixon had sent to herself, about how there was no stalker after all—just a little prank or goof dreamed up by Esther. Then I explained about the property that Phyllis had owned.

"It was about money," I said finally. "Phyllis borrowed the money to buy all these properties. She was basically just a front for somebody else. They must have had a falling-out. So if we find out where the money came from, then we'll know who killed Phyllis. It looks like Esther figured out who she was fronting for. And whoever killed Phyllis then killed Esther because Esther was onto them."

Fontaine scratched his head. "Thought we already knew who killed her. That writer, Patrick What's-his-name."

I shook my head. "I think we were wrong."

"Now you think it's this Shana person?"

I blew out a long stream of air. "Hell, I don't know what I think. She was going to buy into some check-cashing business and this guy who seems to have loaned money or represents somebody who loans money is also connected to this check-cashing company and so I was thinking . . ." I sighed, the connections that had seemed to be so crisply defined only half an hour ago, now suddenly appearing to be pretty tenuous and feeble.

Fontaine looked at his watch. "It's already the weekend. My wife's birthday is today as it happens. Me and her got a table reserved at a nice restaurant in Buckhead."

"I'm sorry."

"You and me have had some dealings, Sunny. I like you and all, you a smart girl, whatnot, okay? But next time you got a . . . would it be safe to call this a half-assed theory?"

"I'm sorry."

"Okay, but next time you get a half-assed theory like this, how about waiting until Monday morning to call. Okay?"

"I'm sorry, I'm sorry, I'm *sorry*."

"Yeah. Well." Fontaine got back in his white Ford and drove away.

The crowd drifted away. Finally it was just me and Loretta Lynn and the firemen. Then the firemen packed up and it was just me.

"All going up in flames," she said.

Then it was just me and the firemen, then just me. An ember glowed in the darkness, faded away to nothing.

I turned and wandered down the street until I reached the burned-out lot where the Blind Pig had been. The whole neighborhood smelled of wet ash now. If things kept up the way they'd been going lately, the whole place would be burned to the ground in another six months. I tromped across the blackened rubble. Looking for something, I guess—though I don't know what I expected to find.

Next thing I knew, I had tripped over something and fallen on my face. I was about used up: my rib was throbbing, I was tired, I felt like a worthless amateur. Ready to go back and take some more codeine pills and lie in my bed for another day or two. Or three.

As my eyes adjusted to the light, I saw what I'd tripped over. Surveyors' string. There were steel pegs driven in the ground, the orange tape on the tops fluttering and disappearing in the headlights of passing cars. They were already preparing to build something else.

I lay there for a while. Something was digging into my elbow. I realized it was a recessed handle—the handle for the trapdoor that opened into the tunnel underneath the Blind Pig. On a whim I decided to go down see if I could find anything of interest there.

I pulled a mini-Maglite out of my purse and opened the heavy door. Although the batteries were a little low, my flashlight still threw off enough light for me to make out the cracked concrete stairs leading down into the darkness.

I went down. Reaching bottom, I found myself in a low tunnel, the walls made of stone, the floor covered with uneven concrete. The whole thing gave the impression of being slapped together in haste. Long fissures ran down the mortar joints in the walls, and there were stones missing here and there in the vault of the ceiling. The tunnel smelled like some rodent had died there recently.

I followed the tunnel about thirty feet. Above me I could hear cars barreling down Boulevard, making the stone walls vibrate alarmingly. I told myself that if it had made it seventy-five years, it would make it a few more minutes before collapsing. But still it was unnerving.

I don't know what I was looking for—if anything. Maybe I was just curious. But my flashlight was good for another few minutes, and here I was, right? So why not see where it led?

The smell of the dead rodent grew fainter as I walked on in the direction that I took to be leading me toward the cemetery on the other side of the street. Eventually I came to another flight of stairs. I walked up, and found myself underneath another heavy slab of concrete—a duplicate of the door on the other side of the street. I supposed this was the one Loretta Lynn had told me about, the one that led up into the cemetery.

I pushed, expecting it to move as easily as the one in the Blind Pig, but it didn't budge. For a moment I had a panicky feeling. You know the kind of thing I'm talking about: what if the trapdoor on the other end closes, too, and I'm trapped down here forever? I heaved away, put as much of my hundred-pound frame into the effort as I could, and when the door wouldn't move even an inch, I hurried back to the other side.

Looking up the concrete stairs I saw stars, sky, lights. No problem: the trapdoor was still open, I wasn't going to die down here, what a relief. I laughed loudly. Silly, worrying about a thing like that. The dead rodent smell was awful.

As I was about to head up the stairs, a thought struck me. If the door on the other end wouldn't open from down here, how had Keith Trice gotten out this way? Maybe he was just stronger than me. Or maybe somebody had sealed the other end of the tunnel since the fire.

As I was thinking, I felt a soft breath of foul-smelling air on my face. A breeze? Down here? It didn't make sense. I narrowed my eyes, pointed the flashlight in the direction the air seemed to be coming from.

Then I saw it: a small rectangular patch of blackness about half way up the wall. What was it? A ventilation shaft of some sort? That seemed unlikely. It wasn't like this was the Paris Metro. A smaller tunnel? Maybe Keith had gotten out through *here*.

I poked my flashlight into the hole. It was about three feet square, a tiny concrete tunnel leading back toward who-knew-where. All I could see were cobwebs and greasy-looking stains oozing down the walls.

Why does a person become a private investigator? I guess in my case it's because I'm inveterately curious. Nosy, if you want to put it that way. Your ordinary sane person would have looked into the dark, stinking, dirty little tunnel and said, "Huh. A dark, stinking, dirty little tunnel." Then they would have walked back up the stairs, closed the trapdoor and walked away.

For good or ill, I'm not built that way.

My heart raced, my skin crawled, and my stomach rose in my throat as I crawled into the tiny space. But I did it. I went.

I'm not claustrophobic, but I'm not wild about tight spaces either. I crawled along with a sort of sick feeling running around inside me. But whatever it was, that compulsive nosiness of mine, it pushed me on. Ten feet. Twenty. Forty. I wasn't sure how far I'd gone, but it seemed like an awful long way. My knees started getting sore and I banged an elbow on a piece concrete that stuck out of a crack in the wall and my broken rib was killing me.

Then the flashlight went out.

I took a couple of deep breaths, clicked the switch a couple of times. Nothing. I banged it on the wall. Nothing. If that pink bunny with the drum had been there, I'd have gladly strangled it.

I looked over my shoulder. Behind me was nothing but darkness. As my eyes adjusted, I saw that in front of me there was some light. Not much, but some. I started heading toward the light as fast as I could crawl.

When I reached the end, with a sinking feeling, I found myself on the wrong side of a steel grate. I pushed, but it was set firmly in the concrete and wouldn't move. I mouthed a few choice words of the sort my mother disapproves, then just sat there for a moment, frozen. There was no way to turn around, so I was going to have to crawl backward into the darkness. It was not a mechanically difficult thing. All I had to do was crawl backward. But psychologically, I realized, I had gone a bit far out on the limb of darkness, disorientation, sore knees, throbbing ribs, tight spaces, cobwebs, and invisible dead rats.

I was nearly in tears. Why did I do this kind of stupid thing all the time? I had a knack for getting myself into places that I wasn't prepared to get out of. Suddenly all I wanted was to be back in my room, drinking Gallo and sucking on a nice Codeine pill.

I guess I panicked, because the next thing I knew I had grabbed on to the steel bars of the grate and started shaking them. To my surprise, though, this time the grate moved, swinging backward into the tunnel with a loud groan of rusty metal. It hadn't moved earlier because I was pushing instead of pulling.

Almost ready to cry with relief, I yanked it all the way open. The hinges shrieked loudly. Then I pushed myself forward, tumbling out the opening and falling a couple of feet onto a hard clay floor.

After I'd quit moaning from the shock to my ribs, I looked around. The chamber into which I'd fallen was about twenty by forty—maybe a little longer, it was hard to tell. The far end of the room faded off into darkness. Above me there was a dull smudge of light: a small dirty window. After a moment, I figured it out. I was in somebody's basement, the old-fashioned kind with a dirt floor and wooden stairs leading up to the main floor of the house.

I looked around. An ancient black furnace hunkered over in one corner of the basement, along with a hot water heater of more recent vintage. There was junk stacked up everywhere. Moldy stacks of *National Geographics*, boxes, bags, a child's rusty bicycle, a grimy old push mower. All the usual castoffs that accumulated in old basements. On the far side of the space was a work bench with some rusty-looking tools hanging over it.

I took a deep breath. The smell was awful. Much as I hated the prospect, I was going to have to get back in the tunnel and crawl back the way I came. Couldn't very well go up the stairs, knock on the door, and say, "Scuse me folks, I just happened to be in your basement, mind if I just let myself out?"

I looked into the black rectangle of the tunnel and took another deep breath. It gave me the willies, thinking about going through there again without a functioning flashlight.

Which is when it struck me: with all the assorted crap down here, maybe I could find a couple of Double A batteries somewhere. The workbench seemed like a good place to start.

I threaded my way through the maze of crap to the workbench. I found some D-cell batteries that looked more or less usable, but of course they were too large. I found cans and jars containing just about every shape and size of fastener manufactured in the world since the fall of Rome. Finally I found one double A battery. I smiled. One battery would be enough.

But when I picked it up, my sense of triumph ebbed away: the acid had wept out one end a long time ago, leaving a puddle of sticky fluid on the wood bench.

I began working my way halfheartedly through the junk. The likelihood of finding a working battery down here, I realized, was nil. I stopped to get my bearings in the dark. I was now on the far side of the basement in the darkest part, the ceiling joists so low that I had to crouch down to keep from banging my head.

The smell had gotten worse.

Behind me was a bare patch of red clay. Most of the clay floor, I had noticed, was dusted with a white powdering of mold. But here the clay was dark. Good old red Georgia clay, freshly turned.

In the middle of the patch of dark clay were two small mounds of dirt, one of them slightly darker than the other. The mounds were about six feet long, three feet wide, rising six inches above the normal grade of the floor. Between the two mounds lay a shovel.

I felt the hair rise on my neck.

Without giving it much thought I grabbed the shovel and started digging. Quietly.

I had gotten about a foot into the mound when the shovel struck something that yielded only grudgingly to the steel blade. I fought back an urge to retch, got down on my knees, and scrabbled in the dirt. I wanted to stop, wanted to get back in that damn tunnel and crawl away, but something in me kept pressing. I had to know.

Two or three weeks of lying under a foot of dirt doesn't do much for the complexion. Doesn't do much for you period. But even with the horrific damage that a couple of weeks of decay had done, I could make out the face of the body I had uncovered.

It was Keith Trice. He had a large hole where the bridge

of his nose had been once been, a hole big enough to let in a nine-millimeter slug.

"Good gracious," a voice behind me said. "What *do* we have here?"

I whirled around. A small dark figure stood on the wooden stairway. I couldn't make out much about him, except that he was holding a gun in his hand.

"Benny?" I said finally.

CHAPTER 30

"ON ONE LEVEL, I'm moderately pleased," the small fat man said.

It was Benny, definitely Benny. And yet somehow *not*.

The small man on the stairs had the same pudgy face, the same pudgy build, the same limp greasy hair, the same Coke bottle glasses, the same worn overalls and cheap shoes. And yet something in him was lit up, animated in a way that the Benny I knew was not. Cunning. Intelligence. Will. Everything that had been absent in the simple little man I'd met in the Blind Pig.

"So how did you figure it out?" the man who seemed to be Benny said.

"Uh. I guess I didn't."

Benny—it had to be Benny—smiled and trotted down the stairs. Then, suddenly, I saw it. The man who had come out of the office, the man I had assumed was Delbert Rathrock, Attorney at Law, was in fact Benny Muse. Take away the pompadour, the Italian shoes, the mohair coat, the paisley necktie, maybe a pair of tinted contact lens—and this was what you had left.

Benny stared at me, his little eyes gleaming in the half light. "You didn't figure it out. And yet, here you are."

"Blind luck, I guess." I didn't know what else to say. What was I going to do? Plead? Tell him he'd never get away with it if he killed me? There was nothing in those hard little eyes that gave me the slightest hope that he had anything in store for me but a bullet in the head.

"Esther didn't tell you?" Benny kept looking at me.

I shook my head.

"She kept nosing around here in Cabbagetown. I got the impression she'd figured it out."

"I don't know. Maybe she did, maybe she didn't. She told me she had, but she never told me her theory."

"Well, this is all very awkward," Benny said. "Nothing personal but I'm afraid I'm going to have to whack you, as our Italian friends would say."

I just stood there shivering.

Benny trotted down the stairs, full of vigor and drive. It was eerily off-putting to see him bounce around like that instead of shambling along the way he'd moved when I met him at the Blind Pig.

When he'd gotten about six feet away, he said, "Turn around, put your hands up on that joist."

I did what he said, my body moving like molasses, my heart pounding wildly. I felt like all my strength had gone away, and was barely able to lift my arms. The clammy splintery surface of the joist felt strangely distant under my fingers.

"Whhh," I said. I was trying to ask some kind of question, but I couldn't get it out. My lips had gone numb, tingling.

"Huh?" Benny said irritably.

"Whhhh."

"Crap," Benny said. I heard him fumbling with the gun. "Don't use these goddamn things much, forgot I had the safety on."

"Whhh," I said again. There was a long pause. In some recess of my mind, I managed to pull a whole thought together. "Long time," I said finally.

"Oh shut up."

"Long time. You been at this a long time. You must want to tell somebody."

Benny snickered sharply. I figured he must have gotten the safety off, but still he hadn't pulled the trigger.

"I mean, God, Benny. What a masterstroke. I don't know what you been doing all these years, but whatever it is, it's damn impressive work."

Still another pause. Then, finally, Benny spoke. "You can't even imagine," he said. His voice was hard, superior. "You can't imagine the discipline it takes."

"Tell me," I said. "You know you want to."

Benny took a long breath. "Man, it stinks down here." I heard him pull back the hammer of the gun. They always say in books that a thing like that sounds loud as a gunshot. But it didn't. In the actual event, it sounded distant, far away, like something from another life.

And suddenly, across all that distance, I sensed that I had him.

After a moment, Benny spoke. "Yes. Yes," he said. "Yes, darling, my life has been a masterstroke." He cleared his throat.

"Go on," I said. "Tell me."

I couldn't see his face, but I knew somehow that he was smiling.

"When I was ten years old, they sent me to the state crazy house over in Griffin. My mama had me committed as an incorrigible. I had been torturing cats, stealing things, you know, run-of-the-mill juvenile delinquency. Then one day I hit the old lady with a baseball bat. Miss Opal." He sneered the words out. "That goddamn ugly drunk whore. You can't imagine what it's like to get sent to the nuthouse when you're just a kid. I mean those were some seriously, righteously *fucked up* people. Howlers, screamers, self-mutilaters, people who smeared themselves with feces, girls who'd put food in their privates. I mean, my God! It was ridiculous. But I have to say this: even as a kid, I realized while I was there that there was in fact something different about me, something different from normal people. Something about me that would never fit in. Anyway, for a while I fought the system at the crazy house. You know how that goes."

He paused. "Well, maybe you don't. A bunch of big sadists beat the crap out of you, nurses shove drugs down your throats, doctors condescend to you. Some of the older kids would sell other kids as punks." There was a long pause. "Well, anyway. Big mess. Very unpleasant.

"Somewhere along the way, though, I had a moment of lucidity. This was just at the tail end of the days when they still did lobotomies, and there was this one kid that came in—I mean, very whacked-out character. Totally violent nutcase. And they gave him the old prefrontal one day, just like in *One Flew Over the Cookoo's Nest*. You remember? Nicholson and Big Chief and all that? Yeah. Great flick. Anyway they gave this kid the prefrontal and he came back all pleasant, easy-going, stupid. Stupid but compliant. And suddenly I saw the light. All the world wants out of Benny Muse is compliance. Comply with the System, and the System will tolerate you. So I started practicing. I'd go over in the corner and just sit. Do nothing at all. After a while I got good at it. What I realized was, Hey, all I had to do was *pretend* to be compliant. Then as soon as the System stops noticing you, shoot, you can do any damn thing you want.

He chuckled briefly. "Can I tell you something, Sunny? Since I'm about to kill you, I guess I can." Another chuckle.

"Knock yourself out," I said.

"One day I was sitting there. Practicing being still. Me and the kid with the prefrontal? We sit there and sit there and sit there. Must have been six, eight hours, barely moving a lick. After a while, the orderlies and the nurses, they don't even see us anymore. It's like we turned into wallpaper. So I reach over, and I put my hand around this kid's shoulder. He doesn't care. Then I put my hand over his mouth. He doesn't move. I put my hand over his nose, squeeze off his air. Well, finally, he reacts. Kind of flops around and stuff? But it's over pretty quick, because by God I'm holding on for dear life. When I'm done, he's gone. Stone dead. Just like Big Chief did to Jack Nicholson in the movie. Only I'm not doing it to be nice or to make some statement about free will or something. Shit no. I'm doing it because I feel like it.

"Then I get up, walk away. They never even asked me about it. Can you imagine that? The more compliant you *seem,* the more you can get away with. Very, very crucial revelation in my life.

"Two weeks later, I go home. Everybody figures poor little Benny must have had a lobotomy or electroshock or something. Time goes by, everybody forgets about crazy, mean, strange, smart little Benny. All they know is Benny the moron. It was great. Got to watch TV all day, didn't have to go to school, didn't have to clean my room, didn't have to do squat.

"Now Miss Opal, my sainted mother, is no dummy. She applies for every kind of government assistance on the planet. Got the social workers doing overtime, finding ways to make a buck off her moron son. AFDC, Social Security disability, state rehab assistance, you name it. Me being a moron was putting nine hundred and fifty bucks of folding money in her pocket every month. That was a lot of money back in the day.

"On my thirteenth birthday, Miss Opal goes out to the mailbox, comes back with my disability check. And I'm standing there with a softball bat in my hand. I tell her, 'Mama, today you're going down to the bank, set up an account for your poor moron son, and my disability check—*my* disability check—goes in *my* goddamn bank account.' " Benny laughed loud and long. "You should have seen that old girl's face! Knowing I'd been playacting for three long years by then and she hadn't even picked up on it? You could have knocked her over with a feather. She didn't want to do it, of course. But I was bigger this time, and when I whacked her a couple times upside the head with that baseball bat, boy, she got real eager to please. I told her, 'None of this incorrigible shit either. You let me do my thing, you put my money in the account like a good girl, I'll give you two hundred bucks a month to spend on booze.

"And that's how we worked it. After a while I started investing in stocks. You'd be amazed, way the stock market's been over the past two decades? I made me a tidy little sum. But over time I started getting restless. Wanted to stretch my legs a little. So I told everybody that I'd gotten enrolled in one of these work programs. You know, rehab for retards? But instead I went up to Georgia State University, took me some courses, got my accounting degree, my real-estate license, so on so forth. Every day, I'd leave the house as Benny the moron, get on the bus, carry a change of clothes in a little backpack. On the other end of the line I'd go into a bathroom, out comes a different Benny. Like Superman in the phone booth."

"But why?" I said finally. "If you've got the self-discipline to do something like that, why not just be normal?"

"Because I'm *not* normal! I *enjoy* picking up that disability check every month. I *enjoy* depositing my dearly departed mother's Social Security check every month."

"You killed her?"

"No. She just died. Went to sleep on the couch, never woke up. Cirrhosis of the liver. That woman was an atrocious drunk. But if I let her get buried, then Uncle Sammie stops sending me her Social Security check. I enjoy getting that check. Makes me feel warm and fuzzy every time I see it." I felt him smiling again. Fondly, almost—or that's the way I imagined it anyway.

I don't know what it was—maybe just the passage of time—but the fear was getting wrung out of me. I'd gotten past the deer-in-the-headlights phase, and suddenly I felt engaged, ready to act. Only, with the pistol at my back, what could I do? I had to play him a little, see if I could get somewhere with him.

"So what does any of this have to do with Phyllis McClint?" I said.

"I'm not without introspective impulses," Benny said. "Sometimes I used to ask myself what made me so different from other people. Did a little reading. Had one of those 'ah-ha' experiences when I was about eighteen, twenty. Reading about criminal personalities. Found out I'm what the shrinks call a highly organized sociopath. I just don't give a shit about other people, don't give a shit about the rules. I just do what I want. But unlike most sociopaths, I'm real smart, real disciplined." He paused. "Putting one over on Uncle Sammie's kind of fun. But a scam like that gets stale after a while. I had all this money, nothing to do with it.

"Phyllis used to come into the Blind Pig, talk to me like I was her pet. Oochie-coochie-coochie. You know how people do that? Talk to their doggie in a silly voice about all kinds of stuff that doesn't mean dick to Fido. 'Oh, he thinks he's just people!' It's so pathetic." A big barking laugh. "Anyway, she'd talk to me like that. Tell me about all this property she wanted to buy, so on, so forth, trying to figure out how she was going to come up with the money to get some property. She used to buy all these tapes off the TV, these no-money-down schemes. You ever see that stuff on cable? The channels that nobody watches? Anyway, finally what I did is I found this disbarred lawyer, fellow by the name of Delbert Rathrock. A wine head, just like my sainted mother, Miss Opal.

"So I got Delbert to be my front man. He sets up this finance company, then he goes to Phyllis, loans her the money to buy these places."

"You're talking about Cabco," I said.

"I thought you said you hadn't figured this out."

"I figured out some of it. But not all."

Benny grunted. "Yeah. Well, anyway, I set up the deals so that Cabco had options on all the property. Buried the option clause in the contracts. Then I went around and did some selling of my own. I knew this place was going to get hot from a real-estate perspective. You could see it coming, four, five years back. So I found some operators who wanted land to build some high-density properties. Condos, fake lofts, that kind of thing.

"I was just about to sew up a deal, twelve solid acres of property here. All I had to do was exercise my options, then I could boot the tenants, flatten half of Cabbagetown, sell out at about quadruple my investment.

"Problem was, just as my deal was about to close, Phyllis shows up and tells Delbert Rathrock she wants to pay back the loan. Turns out she'd raised the money to buy back the loans by cooking up crystal meth for Shana Marks in the Blind Pig. If she pays back the loan, my options on the property go away, my deal evaporates, I'm screwed.

"You were going to get your interest back for loaning her the money," I said. "So what's the big deal?"

"You don't develop a condo out of the blue. You got environmental impact studies, architectural plans, all kind of money you got to sink into it. If she paid off that loan and sold out to another developer, I took a huge beating. Huge."

"Which is when you decided to kill her."

"Correct. And you want to know the beauty part? With her dead, there's nobody to pay the note. I foreclose on the properties, make my deal, get her coming and going, so to speak."

"Yeah, but getting yourself locked up in that place with a guy as unpredictable as Keith Trice? That kept bugging me. Why would somebody do a thing like that."

Benny didn't answer, so I figured I'd better keep pressing, eat up some more time.

"Okay . . . so I'm still curious, Benny. Who *actually* shot Phyllis?"

"Glenn O'Connor."

"Who?"

"The guy in the grave. He's not Keith Trice at all. His

name's Glenn O'Connor. That was all part of the setup. Glenn was a pro. Did hits, heavy collections, transport, stuff like that for some Irish goons up in Boston. He was a pretty doggone good actor, too, wouldn't you say? The guy's actually like twenty-eight years old. Got one of those natural baby faces." He laughed. "Well. Not anymore."

"But why the setup? Why not just make it look like a carjacking or something?"

"I thought about doing it that way. Be less risky, sure. But, *damnation*, it was more fun this way!" He chuckled. "Plus, I got to kill three birds with one stone."

"How so?"

"Well, first off, obviously I get Phyllis out of the way. But, like you say, I could have done that easier. Second, when we set fire to the place, I figure it's a good bet the whole block will go up in flames. That saves me the legal hassles of booting out all the tenants."

"Still. I mean this whole thing was godawful baroque."

"Baroque? I'm not sure I know what that word means. But here's the thing about framing somebody. If you don't do a good job of it, somebody's gonna figure it out. So here's where I was at: I knew this asshole Patrick Triplett was banging Phyllis. I knew him and his wife came down to the Blind Pig every Friday night around midnight and sat at the same table. And Phyllis always came in late to do the night deposit, keep an eye on things.

"So I hired a guy that looked kind of like Patrick—a slightly downmarket client of my amigo Delbert Rathrock—gave him a fake ID with Patrick's name on it. He goes to that pawnshop, buys the gun, fills out the federal form in Patrick's name. I fire the gun once and save the used cartridge, then plant the gun under the table where Patrick and Connie always sit, plant the cartridge behind the basket of jelly on his table. His gun's loaded with MagSafe bullets, right? The slugs that are made of epoxy filled will with tiny lead balls. Then Glenn comes in, shoots three shots in the air, then the lights go out. His gun's loaded with old-fashioned lead slugs. All except the fourth round. That one's one of these high-tech MagSafe rounds. So he shoots the fourth shot at Phyllis. The reason it's a MagSafe is that the state crime lab can't do a ballistic identification on them, can't match a specific round to a specific gun. But it's the exact same kind of round as I loaded in the gun that was planted under Patrick's table."

I mulled the whole thing over for a few seconds. "So wait," I said. "You counted on people sitting right there watching him pull the trigger and yet not being able to testify that they saw him shoot her?"

"All you need is conflicting testimony. A couple people say, 'Oh, sure, it was that Keith Trice guy.' Five people say they were hiding under the tables and didn't see anything. One guy says, 'No, I saw it nice and clear and Patrick was the one who did it.' Now at first the cops are obviously going to assume it was Glenn who did it. Or Keith, whatever you want to call him. But then later when the cops locate the real Keith Trice and he turns out not to be the guy in the restaurant, when it turns out that the round that killed Phyllis turns out to match the cartridge on Patrick's table and not the ones in Glenn's gun, when they start to go over things careful, they start saying, well, hey, maybe it didn't go down like we thought. Plus, here's this little retarded fellow swearing up and down that he saw Patrick Triplett pull the trigger. They would have had to look at the whole thing under a microscope. Eventually they'd have put it all together and decided it was Patrick who killed Phyllis." Benny Muse laughed. "Your being there just speeded things up a little."

"And the tunnel? Keith or Glenn, whoever he is, you had told him about the tunnel, right? So as soon as the place goes up in flames, he scoots."

"That's it."

I thought about it for a while. "Okay, but why frame Patrick? You had the tunnel for Keith to escape from. He could have just shot Phyllis and hauled ass. Why did you need to frame anybody at all?"

"Two things. First, it gave me a way of convincing Glenn O'Connor to pull the trigger, see, because I tell him that in the end the murder is going be blamed on somebody else anyway. So even if the cops catch up with him, he's not looking at the electric chair."

"And the second thing?"

"Remember, Sunny, earlier I said it was *three* birds with one stone."

"Yeah."

"Well, he annoyed me."

"*Who* annoyed you?"

"Patrick! Who you think we're talking about? Patrick figured I'm just some retard, he can make all the jokes about what a bunch of rednecks and fools everybody in Cabbagetown was and it wouldn't bother me. But you know something? It pissed me off, Sunny. I don't like people knocking us Cabbageheads. So framing Patrick, that was just a little game I played. Like scamming Uncle Sam out of a disability check. I just wanted to put him in the crapper for a while, see how he liked it. And if it didn't work, if after looking at all the evidence the cops still concluded that it was Glenn, hey, no skin off my nose."

"Because you were going to kill Glenn anyway."

"Like they say, dead men don't talk."

It was quiet for a while in the foul-smelling basement.

"My God," I said finally, "you probably could have cut a deal with Phyllis, both of you would have walked away rich. Not to mention some poor sap wouldn't be sitting around over at the jail getting charged with a crime he didn't commit."

"No doubt." Benny sucked some air through his teeth. It made a high whining noise, like a punctured bicycle tire. "But like I say . . . that wouldn't have been any fun, would it?"

• • •

I think I've mentioned that I'm kind of a martial arts nut. I teach a self-defense class for women, I've studied a Japanese karate style called Shito-ryu for about fifteen years, and I'm a third degree black belt. Plus I've got collected a few years of aikido and tai chi thrown in along the way. But I've never felt entirely confident about how useful any of this stuff is. People frequently ask me if karate really works on the street. And in my heart of hearts, I've never been sure. Truth is, real violence is crazy and unpredictable, and terrible things can happen in the wink of an eye.

Then there's this: I weigh, on a good day, ninety-eight pounds. A hundred and three if I'm retaining water. Truth is, a good big man is a lot better than a good small woman. I've only been in a couple of physical altercations in my life, but in both of them I came out on the worse end of the deal.

On the other hand, though, none of my scrapes ever really came down to strength or size. Or gender either for that matter.

They had always come down to surprise. Surprise is the great equalizer.

"Benny?" I said.

"What?"

I couldn't see him, but I could hear his voice, getting impatient now. I estimated he wasn't more than three feet away. But then these things are hard to tell. I took a breath and hoped I had gauged things right.

When I whirled around, there was no surprise in Benny's eyes. I didn't give him time for that. In fact, his eyes didn't widen until I had already trapped his gun with my right hand, pulling him off balance and toward me. He *really* got surprised when I hit him in the nose with a picture-perfect palm heel strike. His nose caved in with a sound like a snapping pencil and he grunted softly.

I drove my knee into his groin and he grunted again,

louder this time. Then I put a joint lock on his hand, the one with the gun in it. Aikido practitioners call the lock I used *kote-gaeshi*. I'd never done it on a person with a gun in their hand before. It didn't work like it did in class. In class when you apply *kote-gaeshi,* the other person pats their leg or takes a break-fall and then you let go and the other person jumps up and smiles. In Benny's case, however, it broke his trigger finger, and then he started screaming, as they say, like a girl.

After I kicked him in the face, though, he shut up for the duration.

I have to make a confession. I walked up the stairs and out Benny's front door and down the street, and I didn't think once about the dead bodies in the basement, didn't think about the senseless murder of Phyllis McClint or Esther Nixon, didn't think about what screw had gone loose in some odd little boy's head that had led him down such a weird and horrible and murderous path. All I thought about was that my shit had *worked*. Fifteen years of practice and, by God, it had really worked! I'd opened up that can of authentic Japanese whoop-ass, and look what had popped out! *Yes! Yes! Oh, my God, yes!*

I can't even begin to tell you how good it felt.

So the next person who asks me whether karate works on the street, I'll tell them, *Go down to the death house at the state pen in Reidsville, ask a guy name Benny Muse. See what he thinks.*

CHAPTER 31

I T CAUGHT UP with me eventually of course. I took three months off from work, and Barrington, bless his heart, took an unpaid leave of absence from the Bureau, and we went up to Nova Scotia, rented a cabin with no telephone, no TV, no radio, no lights. Barrington shot a moose and we ate it for months. At first he used to joke about how he was the Great Black Hunter, the One Moose Man, and so on. But then it was moose stew, moose soup, moose jerky, moose casserole, moose burgers, moose, moose, moose, moose, and he got real quiet about his hunting skills.

I sat around and read and stared at the northern lights a good bit. There was a lot of silence, and Barrington put up with it manfully. I didn't practice karate, didn't work out at all. Ladies, don't get jealous, but I didn't gain an ounce. The moose diet, I suppose. Eventually we came home.

I won't say I'm precisely over what happened last winter, but at least I'm not lying around downing Percosets and Gallo. One thing, though? No more moose—never, ever again.

•   •   •

By the time we got back, Patrick Triplett was the American sensation du jour. He'd written this instant book about his experience as a wrongfully accused guy called *The Agony of Innocence*. Or *Agony and Innocence*? I forget. Something pretentious like that. He was on Oprah and so on, and he got a big advance and Tom Cruise is rumored to be playing him in the movie. I haven't read the book, but friends tell me he made me out to be a real horse's ass. Can't say I blame him.

I ran into him at a gallery opening last week, where he was accompanied by a blond undergraduate with fake boobs and black-painted fingernails. He wasn't especially sober, and I'm not even sure he recognized me. We talked briefly, though, and he was very quick to tell me he'd signed a three-book deal with Simon & Schuster to write a bunch of what he called "potboilers about chesty babes and self-satisfied lawyers with chiseled features." The advance for the first book was well into the six figures, he told me sourly. He seemed about to choke on self-loathing.

Poor son of a bitch. I could see the writer's block coming on like an avalanche of freight trains.

And not that I begrudge him the success or anything, but I hope Connie gets every last red cent in the alimony settlement.

CHAPTER 32

A COUPLE OF days ago at a few minutes till five o'clock in the afternoon I went down to the cotton mill in Cabbagetown.

A while later, Loretta Lynn showed up.

We stood next to each other for a long time, staring at the condominium-cum-mill which had risen up from the ground where the Blind Pig had burned down. A bank of dark clouds was heading toward us, a big summer rain coming on, and the wind had started to pick up.

"Just got back from the beauty pollar," she said. Her big black pile of hair was tight as a drum, every curl in place.

"Looks pretty," I said.

There was a long pause. A BMW drove by, downshifting into the curve, then a gleaming Mercedes pulled into the gated parking lot with a screech of brakes. A handsome guy in a tweed jacket and jeans jumped out, hustled up to the front door of the fake mill, and punched a code into the security keypad. A man in a hurry.

"Always figured I'd live and die my whole life in Cabbagetown," Loretta Lynn said sadly. "But I'm beginning to reckon it's come time to scoot."

"Where will you go?"

"Back home, I guess."

"Home? I thought this *was* home."

She smiled slightly. "My great granddaddy and great grandmama, they come from some little old holler up around Boone, North Carolina. In my family we always called that home."

"You ever been there?"

She shook her head. "Nope."

"Got a car?"

"Nope."

I looked at my watch. "Won't take us four hours," I said, gesturing at my old Caddy. "Hop in. Let's go."

She looked at me with an odd, puzzled expression. Then something—sadness? regret? fear?—came down over her eyes like a curtain. She smiled a little. "No, hon. No, bless your heart, but I don't believe I'm up to it. Not just yet."

Then she turned and walked back up the street, the warm wind whipping at her clothes. Everything fluttered and rippled in the warm breeze, everything except her fine black pile of hair, which rose into the air as proud and unmovable as the long-dead chimney of the long-dead cotton mill which towered above her.

Then the rain hit, coming down like a wall of smoked glass, and Loretta Lynn Jones was gone.